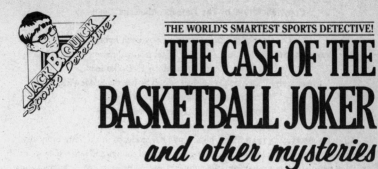

THE WORLD'S SMARTEST SPORTS DETECTIVE!

THE CASE OF THE
BASKETBALL JOKER
and other mysteries

By Karen Gardner

with L. E. Wolfe

A *SPORTS ILLUSTRATED FOR KIDS* BOOK

The Case of the Basketball Joker by Leah Jerome.
The Case of the Stolen Signs and *The Case of the Foiled Fencers* by Max Olson.
The Case of the Puzzling Pounds by K. B. Gardner.
Cover art by Paul Kirchner. Cover design by Martha Sedgewick.
Creative consultation by L. E. Wolfe.
Produced by Angel Entertainment, Inc.

SPORTS ILLUSTRATED FOR KIDS is a trademark of THE TIME INC. MAGAZINE COMPANY

SPORTS ILLUSTRATED FOR KIDS Books is a joint imprint of Little, Brown and Company and Warner Juvenile Books.

Printed in the United States of America

First Printing: October 1990
10 9 8 7 6 5 4 3 2 1

Published simultaneously in Canada by Little, Brown & Company (Canada) Limited

Library of Congress Cataloging-in-Publication Data
Gardner, Karen, 1963—
    The case of the basketball joker and other mysteries / by K. B. Gardner.
        p. cm.— (Jack B. Quick, sports detective ; #1)
    "A Sports illustrated for kids book."
    Summary: Twelve-year-old Jack B. Quick, the world's greatest sports detective, and two friends set out to solve several mysteries.
    ISBN 0-316-72910-8
    [1. Mystery and detective stories. 2. Sports—Fiction.]
I. Title. II. Title : Case of the basketball joker. III. Series.
PZ7.G17925Cas 1990   90-50344
[Fic]—dc20   CIP
                                                                    AC

Contents

The Case of the Basketball Joker

"What's wrong with those guys?" Ollie asked in confusion, running his hand over his hair, which was cut in a high-top fade. We watched the entire Whitman High basketball team climbing all over each other to get to the water fountain.

"They couldn't *all* be that thirsty," Ollie continued. "I mean, they just drank from the cooler." He pointed at the large, round yellow cooler on the bleacher bench below us.

"We better check it out," I said. After all, that was why we were sitting there in the gym at Whitman High School watching the Warriors in the first place. Scott Miller, the team's manager, had left a message on my dad's and my answering machine the night before. He said that someone had been playing practical jokes on the basketball team all week and was totally disrupting the practices. I knew that if the joker wasn't caught soon, Whitman would not have a very good chance of beating undefeated Roosevelt High that

1

weekend. How did I know that? Because I'm Jack B. Quick, sports detective. Ollie Steele is one of my associates.

Ollie and I walked over to the bench, where a few players were sitting and holding towels up to their mouths. "What's wrong?" I asked Tommy Doherty, Whitman's center. "What happened to you guys?"

Tommy looked up at me and I was surprised to see that his eyes were watering. I really didn't think it was anything to cry about.

Tommy opened his mouth as if to say something, then suddenly jumped up and dashed back to the water fountain.

"It must come in waves," I observed. "Maybe it was something they drank. We better check out the cooler."

Ollie was already way ahead of me, busy pouring Gatorade from the cooler tap into a cup before I had even finished my sentence.

"It definitely doesn't smell right," he informed me after sniffing it. Then he took a small sip and handed the cup to me. "It tastes kind of funny," he continued. The next thing I knew, Ollie was sprinting for the water fountain.

I looked at the cup in my hand and then over at Ollie trying to push his way through the group of tall ball players to get a drink of water. I decided that it wasn't necessary for me to try the Gatorade—Ollie's opinion would be enough.

"Hey, Jack," someone called from behind me. "Thanks for coming by."

I turned around to face Scott Miller, our client. "No problem," I responded. "I think we jumped right into this investigation."

Scott shook his head. "I don't know what's going on," he said. "This is getting ridiculous. We haven't been able to get in an uninterrupted practice this week."

"What's been happening?" I asked, looking over my shoulder to see if Ollie's thirst had been quenched yet. I didn't want him to miss this conversation. Ollie was walking away from the fountain. But as he approached me, I could see that his eyes were still watering. That must have been some glass of Gatorade.

"Hey, Ollie," Scott greeted him. "What's wrong?"

"Hi, Scott," Ollie answered. "I fell victim to your practical joker. We've got to find this guy, Jack. Because this time it's personal!" Ollie paused and took a few deep breaths, as if to cool his mouth off. "What was that stuff anyway?"

I sniffed the liquid in the cup again. "I'd have to say Tabasco sauce," I replied. I would not really know what it was for sure unless I tasted it, but this was one time I thought I could make an assumption.

"Back to your question, Jack," Scott said. He pushed his longish brown hair out of his eyes and continued. "I guess the joker first struck about three weeks ago—about a week into the season. Someone put a red sock in the school's washing machine and the team's light blue practice uniforms turned purple. Since then, the joker has been hitting about once a week. But things have gotten much worse the last few days. Yesterday the basketballs were acting really bizarre— bouncing crazily. It turned out that someone had somehow injected water through the air holes. I had to go out and buy

3

some new balls so that the team was able to do their ball drills."

"You have no idea who's behind all these jokes?" Ollie asked in disbelief. "Not even a suspicion?"

Scott shook his head. "I haven't got a clue."

Just then, Coach Teller shouted for Scott. "Sorry, guys, I've got to go," Scott apologized to us as he took off across the gym toward the coach. "I'll talk to you after practice!"

Ollie looked at me and shrugged. "We have nothing to go on, Jack," he said. "Where are we going to start?"

"I don't know," I admitted. We definitely needed some more information before we even had a direction to head in.

"You know, Jack," Ollie continued, changing the subject. "I can't believe how much Scott has grown since last year. He looks as if he's about five inches taller."

"At least," I agreed, suddenly remembering something. "Did he try out for the basketball team again this year?" Scott loves basketball and I knew that he had tried out for the team in both his freshman and sophomore years. But the coach had told him that he really did not have the necessary height to make the team.

"Yeah," Ollie said, picking up a basketball and dribbling it. "I heard he was cut again this year. Something about him being too old to make the J.V. team, which is supposed to be a training ground for the varsity, but not being good enough to make the varsity."

That was interesting, I thought. So Scott was the manager for the third year in a row, and what he really wanted was to be on the team. "It seems to me that we might just have our first suspect," I said to Ollie.

"But he's the one who asked us to investigate," Ollie replied, confused. "Why would he want us snooping around if we were just going to find him out?"

I pushed my glasses up on my nose and scratched my chin. "Well, maybe he just wanted to throw us off," I finally said. "Or maybe he just doesn't think we're that good."

"I guess he's in for a surprise," Ollie said heatedly. He spun around, threw the basketball he was still holding to me and started to stalk across the gym to where Scott was standing with the coach.

"Hang on, Ol," I said, grabbing his shirt. "It's just a theory. We don't know anything for sure yet." Ollie sometimes has a tendency to jump to conclusions and run with them. "Let's start with what we know—the Gatorade."

Ollie looked a little green at the mention of that nasty concoction, but he nodded. "Where should we start?" he asked.

"Do you know where the Gatorade and coolers are kept?" I asked. Since Ollie was on the basketball team at our school, Johnson Junior High, I figured he might know where a team would typically store that kind of thing. I mean, how different can one gym be from another?

"Probably in the equipment room," Ollie answered and headed for a closed door next to the locker room. I followed him, watching as the Whitman team began a three-on-two drill. These players were really good—there was no question about that.

When we got to the equipment room, Ollie turned the

knob and opened the door. I wondered if the door was always unlocked—which would broaden our suspect list considerably—or if the door was always locked except for the times when the team was practicing.

After flipping on the light, Ollie and I stepped into the room. What a mess! Lying all over the place were balls, bats, nets, helmets, uniforms and an ancient pair of football cleats that looked as if they had been in the room since the school opened in 1953.

"This place is disgusting!" Ollie exclaimed. "I thought my room was bad!" He was right—his room at home is bad. But this place was definitely worse.

"What are you guys looking for?" Scott suddenly asked from behind us.

I have to admit, I jumped a little. So I startle easily— lots of famous detectives are like that. It's all in the reflexes. "We were wondering where you keep the Gatorade," I said, after taking a deep breath to calm myself. "We couldn't seem to find it in here."

"Really," Ollie agreed, wrinkling his nose at the mess.

Scott laughed self-consciously. "Yeah, I guess it is out of control in here," he responded. "But what with all these pranks and everything, I just haven't had time to do any cleaning."

"It looks as if this mess was here long before this season started," Ollie muttered softly to himself.

"What?" Scott asked, bending over to pick up a stray sock on the floor. "Here's the red sock that was in the washing machine." He handed it to me.

6

"Listen, Scott," I began, taking the sock and blowing off Ollie's comment. We didn't need to antagonize Scott right now—even if he was our Number 1 suspect. In fact, he was our only suspect so far. I looked at the sock in my hand. It wasn't a very big sock. In fact, it looked like it could be one of mine. "Why don't you just show us where you keep the Gatorade so you can get back to practice," I said, trying to follow the trail of the most recent prank. I could think about the sock later. "I'm sure you're needed out there."

Scott brushed past me and headed for the back of the room. "There's a little refrigerator back here where we keep the Gatorade," he said. "I buy it every Friday for the following week."

"Why Friday?" Ollie asked, stepping out of Scott's way. "Wouldn't it just be easier to buy it on Monday?"

"Friday's practice is usually pretty light because we always have games on Saturdays," Scott explained, uncovering a small refrigerator underneath a pile of track jackets. "So I have more time to run out and pick up the Gatorade. Mondays are usually killer practices and I'm needed here. Besides, the games are the most important, so I definitely have to have enough for everyone to drink on Saturdays."

"All your Gatorade fits in that little refrigerator?" I asked, trying to figure out the capacity in my head. It didn't look possible.

"Every night, I put the next day's stuff in here," Scott explained. "The rest is over there," he finished, pointing at a shelf behind the fridge. There were about 10 bottles of assorted flavors of Gatorade lined up on the shelf. "We're pretty low right now. As I said, I get the stuff on Friday and since that's only two days away . . . "

"How many other teams keep their stuff in there?" I asked, still trying to figure out the fridge's capacity.

"Well, in the fall the football team uses it and in the spring the baseball team does," Scott replied, standing up and heading back toward the door.

"So, only the basketball team keeps their Gatorade in there now?" I inquired. "What about the girls' team?"

"Please," Scott said, curling his lip. "Like the girls even sweat."

Boy, was I glad that Nina Chin, my other associate, wasn't with us right then. It could have gotten really ugly. Nina is not one to stand around and listen quietly to sexist remarks.

"Listen, I've got to get back out there," Scott continued, walking around me. "Do me a favor and make sure you get the light on your way out, O.K.?" And with that, he was gone.

"Phew!" Ollie exclaimed. "I'm glad I'm not on the girls' team here!"

I nodded my agreement, trying to keep my mind on the case. Sometimes Ollie gets distracted from an investigation. "So basically, we have a wide-open field here," I said, running through what we knew so far. "The door is unlocked now and only the basketball team keeps their Gatorade in the refrigerator during the season. Practically anyone could be a suspect. I mean, look at the gym—there must be at least twenty people watching the basketball team practice."

Ollie ran his hand over his high-top fade again. When he did that, I knew he was thinking about our practical joker again. "But we've already got a motive for Scott," he pointed out, his brown eyes serious.

"That's true," I agreed, nodding. "But we haven't got any proof."

We were definitely going to have to come back to practice tomorrow. I really would have loved to catch this joker in the act. Of course, that would be a little too easy. Besides, I love the thrill of the chase.

We walked back into the gym after making sure we turned the lights off and shut the door. The team had started a full-court practice. We sat down on the end of the bleachers to catch the end of it.

"That guy is awesome!" Ollie exclaimed, pointing to a guy who was dribbling the ball up the court. His close-cropped hair was so short he looked practically bald—sort of like Michael Jordan. He was wearing black spandex shorts under his practice uniform and it looked as if he was wearing those "Pump" high tops. I had to admit that, despite all the attitude this guy was sporting, he *was* awesome. He went around the other players as if they were standing still, then he drove up the alley—I won't even mention his hang time—and jammed for two. He slapped hands with his teammates as he jogged down the court.

"Lewis!" Coach Teller yelled, blowing his whistle. "How many times do I have to tell you? We're not on the street here! Get off the playground and get with this team's program!" he concluded with another blast of his whistle.

"Lewis?" Ollie repeated. "That must be Marshall Lewis. He is other-worldly. He averaged 31.6 points a game last season. I hear there were college scouts at most of his games last year, even though he was only a junior."

As I listened to Ollie, I kept my eyes on the action on the court. After the coach reprimanded him, it was as if a light went off in Lewis. He started playing like a machine. Very interesting, I thought, making a mental note of it.

We stayed until the end of practice and then headed home. I told Ollie we had to be back there the next day, but he reminded me that he had a basketball practice of his own. So after I got home, I called Nina. Luckily, she was free. It is always better to have more than one set of eyes at the scene of a possible crime. After dinner, I flipped on my computer. The file I had opened on *The Case of the Basketball Joker* after Scott's call the night before was about to get quite a bit bigger. But in terms of specifics, I really didn't know too much at all—yet.

Δ   Δ   Δ

"Can we get a newspaper first, Jack?" Nina asked the next afternoon as we walked into Whitman High School. She flipped her long black braid over one shoulder and shifted her knapsack to the other shoulder. Nina's the kind of person who worries about carrying her bag on the same shoulder all the time—she says it will permanently curve her spine. As a gymnast, Nina is really concerned with her posture.

"I don't think the paper comes out until tomorrow," I

replied, a little confused—a strange state for me. Since I write for Johnson Junior High's newspaper, *The Eagle*, I know quite a bit about most of the other schools' papers.

"It doesn't," Nina said, grinning. She wouldn't say anything else. Nina loves to keep everyone else hanging.

I didn't ask. I knew I wouldn't get anything out of her and anyway, it would just make her smile even wider if she knew that I was totally curious. So, I just followed her past the gym to the classroom area.

Nina turned and grinned at me as she stopped in front of a door. I looked behind her. *The Whitman Globe* was written in black letters across the front of the door.

"The print shop always delivers the school paper the night before it comes out," she explained. She pushed open the door and we stepped into the newspaper office—and right into the middle of a fight.

"I've been here for four years and I'm sick and tired of the whole thing!" a tall girl was yelling at a blond boy sitting behind a desk in the corner of the office. There were about five other people there and they all seemed to be trying to pretend that nothing was going on. A girl about 10 years old was sitting in a chair behind the angry girl. She looked enough like the older girl for me to surmise that they were sisters. "When are you going to give us the coverage we deserve?" the girl continued. She had long red hair pulled back from her face in a French braid and was wearing black suspender pants and a white T-shirt.

"Listen," the blond guy said, standing up. He only came up to the girl's shoulder. He pushed his round, wire-rimmed

John Lennon glasses up on his nose and continued. "We only have so much space in the paper and we have to give our readers what they want. And what they want to read about is the *boys'* basketball team."

The girl started to say something, but the guy cut her off and continued. "Face it, Holly. That's just the way it is. Girls' basketball is really not that hot a story. I can't do anything about it—that's just the way it is."

"What is *that* supposed to mean, Bill?" Holly asked angrily. "You're the editor of the paper. Of course you can do something about it!"

"Come on, Holly, let's not make a federal case out of this," Bill said, trying to calm the girl down. "We're just a school paper. It's really not that big a deal, is it?"

"That's one person's opinion, isn't it, Bill?" Holly asked, her green eyes practically glittering—and I had thought that was just some literary cliché. "Listen, thanks for all your time. Come on, Lizzie, let's get out of here." And with that, she spun on her heel, grabbed Lizzie's hand, brushed past Nina and me and stormed out of the office.

Bill shook his head and sat down. "Women," he muttered. Then he looked up and saw us standing there. "Can I help you kids with anything?"

"Hi," I replied, extending my hand. "I'm Jack B. Quick."

Shaking my hand, Bill raised an eyebrow. "The sports detective?" he asked.

I have to admit that I kind of like having a reputation that precedes me. I nodded. "We're investigating a series of practical jokes that have been played on the boys' basketball team," I explained. "Do you know anybody who would have anything against those guys?"

"You mean, besides Holly Mulford?" Bill asked, jerking his head in the direction of the door.

Nina and I exchanged glances. It hadn't sounded to me as if Holly had anything against the boys' team—just the newspaper.

"Is it my fault that girls' basketball is not as exciting as boys'?" the blond editor went on. "That girl has a problem with everything. What does she want me to do? Waste three columns on a story that nobody wants to read? I mean, there's a reason why women do not have a professional basketball league and men do. Am I right?"

I could feel Nina stiffen beside me. "Listen," I began, trying to change the subject. All I needed was another battle of the sexes to erupt in the newspaper office. "If you can think of anyone else who might have a reason for wanting the basketball team to lose, could you let me know? I'll be at practice for the next few days."

Bill nodded. "But I still think that Holly is your best bet. She's got a major chip on her shoulder."

I could tell that Nina was getting a major chip on *her* shoulder so I hurriedly asked for an advance edition of the paper. Then I had to practically drag Nina from the office. She was definitely spoiling for a fight. That's another thing about Nina. She takes everything to heart. You have to be able to maintain some objectivity in order to be a good detective. You also have to take offense at nothing—otherwise people will be much less open with you.

Δ   Δ   Δ

By the time we got to the gym, we were too late. The practical joker had already struck.

"What is this stuff?" Marshall was saying, as we walked inside. The star player was sitting on the floor taking off his high tops. The rest of the team was either sitting on the floor with him or on the bench. Not one of them was wearing his sneakers.

"We've been slimed!" Tommy Doherty, Whitman's center, exclaimed. He tipped his high top over and green slime oozed out and dribbled onto the floor.

"MILLER!" Coach Teller hollered suddenly. "What's going on here?! I thought you said you were going to take care of all of these pranks!"

Scott hurried over to the coach. I could see a few heated words being exchanged, but I could not hear a thing. Then, the next thing I knew, Scott was heading our way.

"Jack!" the manager hissed, as soon as he stopped in front of me.

"How are you doing, Scott?" I asked calmly. I know that panic is an easily transferable emotion so I try to make it a policy to remain calm at all times. I would never be able to solve a single case if I did not keep a clear mind.

"Listen, Quick," Scott continued, as if he had not heard me. "I asked you to get involved because I thought you could solve this case. What's taking you so long?"

"We've only had this case for twenty-four hours," Nina suddenly cut in. Nina never lets anyone get away with

14

anything. She is a very valuable associate. "We're professionals, and professionalism takes time."

I nodded. There was really nothing I could add to that.

"I'm catching all kinds of flak from Coach Teller, and I need to have results," Scott went on. The coach then called him over to where the team had gathered with their sneakers in their hands. "I have to go. I've got to figure out how to get that stuff out of their high tops."

"I can't believe that guy!" Nina exclaimed, as we watched Scott stride back across the gym floor. "He's got a lot of nerve."

"He's under a lot of pressure," I commented absently. "Let's wait around for a while and see if anything else develops."

We sat down and Nina started leafing through *The Whitman Globe*. In a few minutes, the players came back to the court and the coach led them through a few warm-up exercises.

"I thought you said Marshall Lewis is an incredible player," Nina suddenly remarked.

"He is," I replied, startled. That was the last thing I had expected her to say. "He was awesome in practice yesterday."

"Then why hasn't he played in the last two games?" Nina asked, holding up the paper so I could see the article.

"What!?" I uttered in disbelief. The coach must have been crazy not to put Marshall in. He was the kind of player who could change the whole outcome of a game just by walking onto the court—kind of like Michael Jordan.

"It says here that Marshall Lewis was benched for three games, including the one this weekend," Nina replied, reading from the article. "Something about being continually late to practice."

That was interesting, I thought. I wondered how Marshall was taking it. It also could not make him too popular with the team. I mean, the other players must have known that he could make or break them and if he was messing up and not coming to practice on time, that could definitely hurt the team. I was going to have to talk to Marshall after practice.

"There's a major article in here about the game against Roosevelt this weekend, too," Nina went on. "There is a big chart comparing Jimmy Dalton, Roosevelt's star point guard, and Marshall."

"Isn't that kind of silly?" I asked, a little confused. "If Marshall's benched, what difference does it make how they match up?"

"You got me," Nina answered, shrugging her shoulders. "Maybe the writer, Jeff Daniels, thinks the coach will change his mind about the benching if he sees this article. Jeff goes so far as to say that the Warriors don't have a prayer against Roosevelt without Marshall. I'd say that was laying it on the line."

Nina handed me the paper. I scanned the article. It was pretty obvious that Jeff Daniels was trying to persuade the coach to let his star guard play. Meanwhile, Whitman's reporter had actually gone over to Roosevelt to interview Jimmy Dalton. Jimmy sounded like a major ego freak.

"We're going to crush the Warriors!" was one of his actual quotes. He also said that Whitman didn't stand a chance—even with Marshall playing. I believe that confidence in one's ability is a good thing, but this was ridiculous.

"You know," I said to Nina, a thought suddenly striking me. "Jimmy Dalton is going to lose face, major face, if Roosevelt doesn't win this weekend."

Nina nodded, agreeing with me.

"That makes his stake in the game pretty big," I continued. "I wonder how far he would go in order to ensure a Roosevelt victory."

Nina's eyes lit up as she caught on to where I was heading. "I think we should probably talk to him, don't you?" she asked.

I agreed with her and we sat silently watching the remaining half hour of practice. Mulling over what I knew about *The Case of the Basketball Joker* so far, I came to the conclusion that it was still pretty wide open. The list of suspects was growing, but I had no real leads. It was all a little frustrating.

After practice, I followed Scott into the boys' locker room. Although Nina wanted to come with me, she wasn't permitted to.

"Scott, do you have a second?" I asked, when I had caught up with him.

"Sure, Jack," he answered. "Listen, I'm sorry about what happened in the gym, but this whole thing is making me crazy."

"That's O.K.," I said, and I meant it. I've noticed that

people do funny things when they are under stress. "I was wondering how our joker could have gotten the slime into everyone's sneakers. Do you have any ideas?"

"I guess somebody must have done the deed when we were in the wrestling room."

"What were you doing in the wrestling room?" I asked, puzzled.

"Well," Scott began with a sheepish look on his face, "the coach got into this yoga thing last summer and he wants to get the team mentally strong, so we have half an hour of yoga before every practice."

"Yoga?" That was definitely a new one on me. I mean, I had been around the block a few times, but this was the first time I had ever heard of any high school coach using yoga to boost the team's mental toughness. Not that I have anything against yoga—in fact I'm all for it. It sounds kind of cool. I was going to have to look into it, that was for sure.

Scott nodded. "Yeah, we leave our shoes outside the room—because it's wall-to-wall mat—and . . ."

"*You* do it, too?" I asked, cutting him off.

"The coach thinks it's good for *everyone*," Scott retorted defensively.

Phew! I thought. He was more than a little sensitive about the fact that he was just the manager of the team. Time to change the subject. "So, the team noticed the slime after the yoga session?"

"You got here right after we went back in the gym," the manager answered, a little more calmly. "And that's when everyone noticed."

"And everyone's sneakers had slime in them?" I asked him next.

"Yup, even *mine*," Scott replied. This was definitely a touchy subject.

"Do you have any idea if a lot of kids are still in the school building while you guys are in the wrestling room?" I asked, trying to see if I could narrow my suspect list. I also wanted to distract Scott. It wasn't my fault he hadn't made the team, after all.

"Sure," Scott replied, scratching his head thoughtfully. "We start our yoga right after school, so I'm sure that a lot of people are still hanging out then."

Well, that really narrowed things down. But Scott was right—probably anyone in an after-school activity or sport was still roaming the halls. That didn't help me at all. "Do you know what the slime was?" I went on, trying a different tack.

"Yeah," Scott said, nodding. "My kid brother has the stuff. It's the stuff from that movie all the little kids are seeing. You can probably get it at any toy store."

That wasn't much of a lead, I thought. Scott turned to head into the coach's office. "Before you go, Scott," I said, stopping him. "Could you tell me anything about the circumstances surrounding Marshall's benching?"

"Uh . . . sure . . . " the manager began, looking around the locker room. I could hear the water running in the shower on the other side of the lockers and the guys yelling back and forth to each other. "Maybe we should go into the office," Scott suggested.

"So, what happened?" I asked as soon as the two of us were alone in Coach Teller's office. I looked around while waiting for Scott to answer. The coach was definitely not a neat freak. There were papers lying on every available surface—I couldn't even tell you what color his desk was because it was so piled up with stuff. Two of the four file cabinet drawers were open, and papers and folders were lying on top of them. I peered at some of the clippings hanging all over the walls. Some were so yellow that they looked as if they went back to the coach's playing days.

"Well, there's really not much to tell," Scott said. "Marshall was late for practice six times during the last three weeks. And he wouldn't tell the coach why. He just gave Coach Teller a lot of lip—as usual. So the coach benched him for three games."

"I read Jeff Daniels' article that will be in tomorrow's paper," I revealed. "He seems to think that Whitman doesn't have a prayer without Marshall. Is the coach really going to take that chance and keep his superstar out of the game?"

"That's the problem," Scott answered. "He really is a superstar, and he's got the ego to match. But to answer your question, no. The coach is going to put Marshall in after the tip-off, so Roosevelt will be totally surprised. No one is expecting Marshall to play, not even Marshall himself."

"Why not?" I asked, confused. "I would think the coach would want Marshall to be prepared to play—at least mentally."

"The coach wants to make him suffer a little, so to speak," Scott explained. "Besides, Marshall is always ready to play ball, so I don't think he'll have any problems mentally."

It sounded to me as if the coach and Marshall had had some run-ins before, especially if Coach Teller wanted to make him suffer now. I remembered what had happened on the court in practice the day before, after Marshall had jammed. There definitely seemed to be a personality conflict there. I thanked Scott for his help and left him with his stats in the coach's office. I had to go look for Marshall.

I caught up with the standout guard by his locker. Marshall was sitting on the bench, wearing a pair of jeans and pulling on a pair of cross-training sneakers.

"Marshall Lewis?" I asked, even though I knew perfectly well who he was.

He looked up at me. "Yeah," he said. "Do I know you from somewhere?"

"I'm Jack B. Quick," I answered, offering him my hand. My father always tells me that you can learn a lot about people from the way they shake hands. Marshall had a pretty firm grip. Of course, I'm not really sure what that means, but my dad says it means a lot.

"Jack B. Quick," Marshall repeated, his eyes narrowing. "The sports detective? Did Coach send you in here to find out where I was when I was late for practice? I already told him it was none of his business. And it's none of yours, either!"

Marshall stood up and pulled his shirt out of his locker. He thrust his arms into it and starting buttoning furiously.

"Actually," I began, "I'm investigating the pranks that

21

someone has been pulling on the basketball team for the past few weeks."

Stopping mid-button, Marshall looked at me with a startled expression on his face. I guess he was beginning to realize that the world did not really revolve around him, and that there were other problems more pressing to the basketball team than his tardiness. "What?" Marshall asked.

"I'm investigating the pranks that someone has been pulling on the basketball team," I repeated. "I was wondering if you had any ideas about who might go to such lengths to disrupt your practices?"

Marshall started buttoning his shirt again and looked thoughtful. "Do we even know if this joker wants to disrupt the season, or just the game this weekend?" he finally asked.

My mouth dropped open in surprise. I hadn't even thought that someone could be out to ruin the whole season. But it was still possible that the joker only cared about this particular game. Marshall had definitely opened a can of worms.

"I think it makes a lot of sense that the game against Roosevelt is the target," I said, scratching my chin. "The incidents *have* been escalating this past week." Besides, the suspect list would be a lot smaller if ruining *one* game was the goal of our basketball joker.

"Well," Marshall began, "I can't think of anybody who really wants us to lose besides Roosevelt."

"Jimmy Dalton?" I probed. I wanted to find out how Marshall felt about Jimmy—if they were antagonistic, that sort of thing.

Again, Marshall shocked me. He laughed. "That guy sure *talks* a good game, doesn't he?" Marshall asked. "He's got no substance."

As we continued our conversation, Marshall voluntarily told me that he had missed practice because he was being tutored in math. He didn't want anyone to know about it. And he said that the coach had never given him a chance to explain.

I had begun to revise my opinion about Marshall's attitude when Coach Teller suddenly appeared. Before my eyes, Marshall seemed to turn into a different person—he had major attitude.

"Lewis!" Coach Teller barked from the end of the row of lockers.

Marshall sat down slowly and started tying his shoes. He didn't even look up at the coach.

"Lewis!" the coach yelled again, walking toward his star player. "I'm talking to you!"

Marshall stood up and pulled his gym bag from his locker. "Well, I'm holding my breath, waiting for you to continue," he said sarcastically.

Coach Teller sputtered for a minute. "You may be a good player, Lewis," he hissed, "but you really are lacking in people skills!"

Marshall laughed, but not the laugh I had heard before. Deciding it was time for me to go, I gave Marshall a little wave and walked out of the locker room. The girls' basketball team was just starting its warm-ups when I went to collect Nina. I didn't need to be a detective to know that

Coach Teller and Marshall did not get along—at all. It seemed to me that Whitman's star player went out of his way to annoy the coach. I wondered just how far he would go.

Δ　　Δ　　Δ

After Nina and I got back to my house, we went up to my room. I filled her in about what had happened in the locker room and flipped on my computer. "I think we should check out Jimmy Dalton tomorrow," I began. "Marshall says he's all talk, but I want to find out whether Jimmy has a real motive for making sure Whitman loses." After opening the file on my computer, I started typing in what I had learned that afternoon. "And what about Marshall Lewis?"

Nina agreed about Jimmy. "I don't think Marshall had anything to do with those jokes," she said. "It's just a feeling—call it women's intuition."

I was having the same feeling—but I definitely didn't call it *women's* intuition. It was my detective's intuition. And it was screaming at me that Marshall wasn't behind the pranks.

Anyway, after Nina had left for dinner, I called Ollie and brought him up to date. He said he wanted to go with Nina and me to talk to Jimmy the next afternoon, so we made plans to meet after school and walk over to Roosevelt together.

Δ　　Δ　　Δ

"What is that shaved into the back of his head?" Nina asked, squinting at Jimmy Dalton the next afternoon as we sat in the bleachers watching Roosevelt practice. Jimmy's hair was cut in a high-top fade like Ollie's. But around the back of his head, a barber had shaved something.

"It looks like a bouncing basketball," Ollie said. "See the dotted lines that go up and down and end up at that ball?"

I squinted at the back of the guard's head and then shook my head. What was I doing? I was here to check out a lead, not a haircut.

The Roosevelt team looked pretty sharp as the players ran through a bunch of three-on-two drills. And Jimmy Dalton was good. But not nearly as good as Marshall Lewis, that was for sure.

"Marshall definitely has this dude beat!" Ollie suddenly exclaimed, echoing my thoughts. Jimmy Dalton just didn't stack up. Even if he was wearing those all-plastic, wrap-around sport glasses, like the ones Kareem Abdul-Jabbar once wore and James Worthy of the Los Angeles Lakers wears now.

We caught up with Jimmy heading out of the locker room after practice. "Excuse me!" Nina called, practically running after him.

He turned around and stopped, looking at Nina quizzically. "Yeah, what?"

"My name is Jack B. Quick," I butted in, stepping forward to introduce myself, "and this is Nina Chin and Ollie Steele."

"So?" he asked sarcastically. And everyone thought *Marshall* had an attitude problem.

"We're investigating a series of practical jokes that someone has been pulling on the Whitman High Warriors over the past few weeks," Nina said bluntly. She hates beating around the bush and is always the first one to cut right to the heart of a matter. "We were wondering if you know anything about them."

Jimmy switched his gym bag from his left hand to his right and took a step toward Nina. Great, I thought. Now, we're going to get hurt. "What are you saying?" he asked instead.

"We just wanted to know if you had heard about the jokes or anything," I said diplomatically.

He thought for a minute, and then just said, "Yeah." He paused again. "Word gets around."

"So, you must also know that Marshall Lewis is benched for the weekend," Ollie put in, stepping in front of Nina. That was definitely a good move. Ollie is pretty big for his age.

"Yeah," Jimmy repeated. He was no mental giant, I thought. "They don't have a prayer now," he said. "Not that they had much of a chance before. I was ready for Marshall." He squinted at Ollie. "Don't I know you from somewhere?"

"Maybe you know my cousin, Wells Douglas," Ollie replied. "Lots of people say we look alike."

"Yeah," Jimmy said yet again. "Plays football at Central, right?"

Ollie nodded.

"Anyway, kids, I don't know anything about any pranks being played on the Warriors," Jimmy went on, shifting his gym bag again. "It's a real shame, though." Then he laughed and, with that, he was gone.

We looked at each other and shrugged. Marshall was

like an angel compared to Jimmy. Coach Teller didn't know how easy he had it.

Δ   Δ   Δ

By the time we got back to the Whitman gym, the girls were already practicing. "I guess we missed practice," Nina said, noting the obvious.

We were the only spectators in the gym except for Holly's sister, Lizzie. She was sitting at the end of the bleachers reading a book.

"I wonder if anything happened?" I mused aloud.

"Well, here comes Scott," Ollie said, pointing behind me. "Why don't you ask him?"

"This is getting absurd!" Scott exclaimed as he walked up to us. The veins in his forehead were popping out and twitching so furiously, they looked as if they were going to burst at any second.

"What happened?" I asked, trying to calm him.

Just then, a group of players came out of the boys' locker room. "I can't take it anymore," Tommy Doherty was saying. "I don't know what's going to happen if these pranks don't stop . . . "

"Really," Dan Kovaleski agreed, cutting his teammate off. "It's getting so out of hand, my concentration is totally gone—and you can forget about intensity."

"What happened?" I repeated my question. Things did not look good. I had to solve this case—and quick.

"Someone put itching powder in some of the players' shorts!" Scott exclaimed, shaking his head in disbelief.

Ollie groaned, probably empathizing with how the

players had felt when they had pulled on their shorts. Nina snorted and then clamped her hand over her mouth to keep from laughing. I could definitely see the humor in this prank, but Scott was obviously taking it very seriously. He gave a look that shot daggers at Nina.

"How could that have happened?" I asked, trying to get my associates back on track.

"Well," Scott began, taking a deep breath, "someone probably did the deed when the uniforms were sitting in the laundry basket outside the coach's office after they were washed."

And, I thought in frustration, the locker room was open all day long and guys kept going in and out during gym class.

Scott said he had to run if he was going to catch his ride, and told us that we *had* to solve this case.

"This is getting totally out of hand!" Ollie exclaimed after the Warriors' manager had left. "We're no farther along in this case than when we started." He sighed dramatically.

"We can't give up yet," Nina cut him off firmly. "We cannot let this case get the best of the Jack B. Quick Detective Squad."

I nodded in agreement and looked at the basketball court, thinking over the case. The girls' team was doing three-on-two drills. Holly Mulford was truly a dominating player. She was all over the place. "You know," I mused out loud. "I never did get a chance to talk to Holly."

"That's right!" Ollie responded, enthusiastic once again. Ollie really is a man of motion and he gets kind of down when we don't have a plan of action.

We decided not to wait for the practice to be over because it would be dark by then, so instead we made plans to come back the next afternoon and catch Holly before practice began. We were really cutting it close now. The game against Roosevelt was only a few days away. We had to crack this case soon—before it was too late.

Δ   Δ   Δ

"Listen," Holly said curtly the following afternoon, "I really don't have any idea who's pulling those pranks—and I really don't care."

I exchanged a look with Ollie. (Nina was stuck at a Biology Club meeting that afternoon—so it was just Ollie and me.) Holly was being awfully defensive. I had only asked her if she had heard about the pranks. I had not even inquired whether she had any idea who might be behind them.

"Maybe you should check out Jimmy Dalton," Holly went on, completely contradicting herself. "It seems as if he has the most to gain by putting the Warriors out of commission."

"Well, you would think so," Ollie said. "But I think the Roosevelt players think they're guaranteed to win as long as Marshall is out of the picture."

"That's true," I agreed. "It would be like overkill on Roosevelt's part. Without Marshall, the Warriors are just another good basketball team. With him, they soar."

"Listen," Holly began angrily, "I really have no clue who's been pulling all these pranks and if you think that *I* had anything to do with them, then you're sadly mistaken. I resent the implication that I would do something so . . . "

"Whoa! Wait a minute!" Ollie suddenly cut in. "Did we accuse you of anything?"

"I just wanted to know if you had any ideas," I added. My eyes narrowed in concentration. As far as I could see, there was no reason for Holly to be reacting the way she was.

"I know you kids were in the newspaper office the other afternoon," Holly replied, not lightening her tone at all. "But even though I'm not happy with the newspaper coverage or our practice time slot, I'm not about to play a bunch of stupid, immature tricks to get my way. I'm a little too old for that sort of thing. So why don't you guys just leave me alone!" And with that, Holly turned on her heel and stalked off toward the girls' locker room.

Ollie and I sat down on the bleachers. "She's definitely hiding something, Jack," he said, rubbing his high-top fade. "Hey, do you think I should get something shaved into the back of my head?"

I shook my head. It is unbelievable how Ollie can change subjects in the same breath like that. "She is definitely hiding something," I began, "but I don't know if she's the culprit. It doesn't feel right." I paused and looked at the back of Ollie's head which was still turned around. "And yeah," I said, answering his question, "you should definitely get something shaved into your head."

Just then, Lizzie Mulford walked into the gym. She came over to where we were sitting and stopped. "Have you seen my sister?" she asked. Up close, she looked even more like her older sister—the same red hair, green eyes, freckles and classic bone structure. And, although she was only 10, she was already taller than I am.

I explained that Holly was in the locker room and that she was a little upset with us.

"What for?" Lizzie asked, plopping herself down next to Ollie.

Ollie filled her in. I was just thankful that he didn't ask her if she thought he should get his head shaved.

"Well, can you blame her?" Lizzie asked, her eyes blazing. I guessed that Lizzie had the Mulford temper as well. "Holly's a great player—she deserves better than this! It's totally unfair that that stupid paper only writes a paragraph about the girls' games and a whole spread on the boys. Why don't that many fans come to the girls' games? And I hate waiting so long for their practice to start!"

"Why are you here every day, anyway?" Ollie asked, cutting her tirade short.

"My parents work, and Holly picks me up after school," Lizzie explained, calming down a little. "I go home with her after practice. Besides, I can get a lot of homework done here."

Lizzie talked to us for a few more minutes. Then she headed to the top of the bleachers and pulled a few books out of her knapsack. Ollie and I hung out for another half hour after that. When we left, I noticed that Lizzie was lost in one of her books.

$$\Delta \qquad \Delta \qquad \Delta$$

I hate it when I go to sleep with unanswered questions on my mind. I usually can't make it through the night without waking up. That night was no exception. I jerked awake at 3:00 A.M. with the feeling that I was missing something very important—something really obvious. There were so many suspects floating around in this case, and I had not been able to discount any of them for sure—not even Scott. I tossed and turned for a little while and then gave up. Walking over to my desk, I flipped on the light and the computer.

Scrolling through the file, I read every little thing over very carefully. It had to be there—the one elusive clue that I kept missing. It had to be there . . . and it was! Suddenly, everything made sense. I knew who the culprit was in *The Case of the Basketball Joker*! I couldn't wait to talk to Ollie and Nina.

Δ Δ Δ

"You figured it out?" Scott asked during the last practice before the Roosevelt game. "You really did, Jack?"

"Yup," Ollie said, answering for me. I love to figure these cases out, but I'm not really one to toot my own horn.

"Well, who is our joker?" Scott asked impatiently. "What are you waiting for?"

"For her," Nina cut in, pointing at Holly Mulford who was walking over to us.

"Holly?!" Scott exclaimed. "I should have known."

I didn't bother to correct him, but waited until Holly sat down next to us.

"What do you guys want?" she asked brusquely. "I told you yesterday that I had no idea who your joker could be."

"We think you do," Nina said, without beating around

the bush. Sometimes it is very useful to have such a blunt associate.

"Why don't you tell us who you *really* think our joker is," I added gently, smiling at Holly.

"I don't know what you're talking about!" Holly exclaimed.

I pulled out the red sock that Scott had found in the washing machine. "Do you know whose sock this is?" I inquired, handing it to her.

Holly took the sock silently. "I can't believe it," she said softly. "I mean, I suspected . . . but I didn't think she would go this far."

"Who?" Scott asked, a little confused. "Who are you talking about?"

Just then, Lizzie walked into the gym. She spotted Holly and headed over to us.

"Lizzie, how could you do this?" Holly asked, waving the sock in front of her little sister's face. "Why?"

Lizzie's face practically crumpled in front of our eyes. I never thought that I would ever see someone's face crumple. I had only read about it—another literary image brought to life.

"I'm sorry, Holly," Lizzie blurted out. She started sniffling a little. "I didn't want to get you in trouble." Lizzie wiped a tear from her eye. "I was just so mad that the boys' team got everything, and you're so good . . . "

"Oh, Lizzie . . . " Holly began, and put her arms around her little sister. "Everything will be all right."

Nina, Ollie, Scott and I exchanged looks and stood up.

We walked to the other end of the bleachers.

"Well, now that you have your basketball joker," Ollie asked matter-of-factly, "what are you guys going to do about it?"

"I don't know," Scott admitted. "I guess I'll have to talk to the coach. But I don't think he'll be too hard on Lizzie. She's just a kid."

"And she had a good motive," Nina put in. "The girls' team really seems to get the short end of the stick here. I mean, the least you guys can do is rotate practice time slots or something."

"I suppose that's true," Scott said thoughtfully. "I never really gave it much thought before. I just assumed that the girls were happy with everything. Maybe I could even make room in the fridge for some Gatorade for them."

Nina nodded happily. She hates to see girls' teams not get the same breaks as the boys—even more than Ollie and I do. "Do you have something to add, Jack?"

"Just those two words that give me such happiness," I answered, and then paused a little dramatically. "Case closed."

The Case of the Stolen Signs

"I didn't think we were ever going to get here!" Nina Chin, my associate, exclaimed, as we climbed up the bleachers to the few empty seats left at the top.

I nodded, as did my other associate, Ollie Steele, as we squeezed past a bunch of people and sat down. The three of us make up the Jack B. Quick Detective Squad, and I'm Jack. I looked around the baseball field and took a sip of the soda we had picked up as soon as we had parked our bikes. Luckily, the players were still warming up. I had been afraid we were going to miss part of the action.

"This is going to be a great game!" Ollie exclaimed enthusiastically.

I had to agree with him. The Millhouse Muskrats were playing the Central Vikings for the Eastern Division Championship. The winner would go on to play in the Washington County High School Championship, a best of three series starting on Thursday, against the Roosevelt Tigers. The

Muskrats had won the last three championships. They were the closest thing Washington County had to a dynasty—and I was hoping for Number 4 this year.

The Muskrats are a well-organized team with a former minor league catcher, Buddy Branson, as their coach. Buddy always teaches his team solid fundamentals and a great deal of baseball strategy. His kids usually out-play and out-think all the other teams in the league.

Pitcher Jeff Robbins was at the top of his form during warm-ups. Of course, he wasn't practicing at full capacity, but every one of his pitches went right up the middle of the plate. After Jeff's warm-up, I had no doubt that the Muskrats would win.

About five minutes later, the umpire signaled for the game to get underway. The players had their brief team meetings and team cheers, and then the Muskrats ran out to take the field. Jeff struck out the first three Viking batters he faced. The Muskrats were also three-up, three-down in the first inning. Finally, in the bottom of the second, they got a man on first base: Jon Polk, the third baseman and leading base stealer for the Muskrats. When the next batter came up, Jon sprinted for second as soon as the ball left the pitcher's hand. But the catcher jumped up practically before he caught the ball and threw Jon out.

The crowd sighed as Jon walked back to the dugout. I thought it was weird that he had been thrown out, because he was so quick. Then again, you can't win them all.

Jimmy Hendy, the leftfielder, was up next. He also got a base hit, dropping one between the first baseman and the rightfielder. The next batter, Mike Zemansky, executed a sacrifice bunt in order to advance Jimmy. However, the first and third basemen had moved in toward the plate even before Mike had connected with the ball. The Vikings made a double play to end the second inning. It was really strange—as if the Vikings had known that Mike was going to bunt.

By the fifth inning, it seemed obvious that the Vikings had figured out the Muskrats' signs, or maybe, as Ollie suggested, that someone had given the Vikings the signs.

Sometimes in the middle of a game, the coach needs to tell his players to do something and he doesn't want to call a time-out. So he will signal with pre-arranged signs when he wants them to steal a base or bunt or do something else a little bit out of the ordinary. These signs are often complicated so that no one from another team can figure them out. Last summer, my coach had this sign for stealing that took almost a full minute just to do—he rubbed his hand on his right thigh, scratched the back of his left knee, took off his cap, ran his fingers through his hair, put his cap back on, pulled up his pants a little and re-tied his left shoelace. Nina always said that it looked as if he was doing some strange tribal dance.

In the middle of the ninth inning, the score was tied at 2-2. This was very strange, as the Muskrats were usually ahead by four runs at this point in the game. They were clearly the better of the two ball clubs, yet the Muskrats were only able to put one more run on the scoreboard, eking out a 3-2 victory. Clearly, something odd was going on.

As Ollie, Nina and I were unlocking our bicycles, Jeff Robbins approached us. "Hey, Jack!" he called.

"Hi, Jeff. You threw some great pitches today," I said. Jeff is an amazing pitcher—the best I've seen in high school. He's tall and thin, and Ollie says that he looks like that singer Bobby Brown.

"Thanks, but I think the team has a problem," Jeff said, looking really concerned. "We think someone is stealing our signs. Every play we signaled today was picked up by the Vikings. That can only mean one thing: they know what our signs are.

"And if the Vikings know," Jeff went on, "what's stopping the Roosevelt Tigers from finding out in time for the championship playoff this weekend?"

"Yeah, we noticed the Vikings' 'alertness,' " I said, for lack of a better word. I would never come right out and accuse someone of cheating unless I had proof. "So, I guess you would like our help?"

"We certainly would," Jeff said. "My coach is waiting to talk with you over in the dugout."

"Well, guys," I said to my associates, "let's go see what we can do." We re-locked our bicycles and followed Jeff over to the other side of the field.

"Coach," Jeff called, descending into the dugout. "This is Jack Quick. Jack, this is my coach, Buddy Branson." The coach is a middle-aged man with a receding hairline. What's left of his hair is turning silver, and he's not very tall. In fact, Ollie is almost a full head taller than he is, but Coach Branson is rather stocky.

"Jack *B*. Quick," I said, correcting Jeff, as I shook the coach's hand. I can be really sensitive about the "B." "These are my associates, Nina Chin and Ollie Steele. So, Coach Branson," I continued, getting down to business, "you believe that someone is stealing your signals?"

"Yes," he said, rubbing his forehead. "It's darn obvious that someone knows what the signs are. Did you see the game today?"

"Yeah," Ollie said with a sigh. "We saw it."

"I hate to think someone on my team could be giving up our signs, but I have to know," the coach went on.

"What makes you think it's someone on the Muskrats?" I asked. Buddy Branson paused for moment.

"I don't know," he finally replied. "Who else would know our signals?" He definitely had a point there, I thought. "Regardless, I want to find out who's stealing them and why—before we play the Tigers."

"We'll get right on it, sir," I said, flashing my most confident smile. Not to brag or anything, but the Jack B. Quick Detective Squad has a pretty good track record. I have never met a case I couldn't solve.

"I'm glad Jeff here suggested we use your squad. According to the papers, you're the Dick Tracy of sports," the coach answered.

"We'll do our best, sir," I stated. "I'd like to start by asking you a few questions."

"Shoot."

"Well, first," I said, jumping right in, "do you have any idea who might be responsible?"

The coach shook his head before he answered. "No, not really. The only name I can come up with is Kyle Sampson."

"Kyle?" Jeff asked in an astonished voice. "What makes you think Kyle did it?"

"Well," the coach began, "he's been bad-mouthing me ever since I kicked him off the team."

"You kicked him off the team?" Nina asked. "Why?"

"He was a good ballplayer and all, but he was no team player," Coach Branson said. "He wouldn't follow my signs, ever. It's not easy kicking someone off the team, but I had to do it."

"Do you think he wants revenge?" Nina asked, continuing with her line of questioning.

"Who knows?" he said, shrugging his shoulders. "That's your job. But he could be the culprit."

"That's all you can come up with?" Nina went on bluntly.

"That's it," Coach Branson replied, as much to the point as my associate. "Well, I have to get going. Thanks for helping us out, you guys. I imagine I'll be seeing you again." With that, he got up and walked off to the parking lot.

"Coach Branson!" I called and ran to catch up with him. "Can I have a copy of the team roster?"

"Sure. Here, take this one," he said, pulling one from his clipboard. "I have more in my briefcase."

"Thanks," I said, and walked back to the dugout.

"What about you, Jeff?" Ollie was asking when I returned. "Have any ideas?"

"No," he stated, "but I do know that Kyle wasn't too

happy about being kicked off the team."

"I wouldn't be too happy either," Nina blurted out, "but I don't think I would pull a trick like this to get revenge."

"I'd be really mad," Ollie suddenly said. "If I was kicked off a team, I'd—"

"All right, Ollie," I stopped him before he went off the deep end with fantasy revenge scenarios. "So," I said turning my attention back to Jeff, "you think it was Kyle too?"

"I think he has the motive, yes," Jeff responded, "but I'm not so sure he would do something like this."

"Why not?" Ollie asked, throwing a baseball up in the air and catching it with the other hand.

"I think Kyle would take his revenge in some other form," Jeff explained. "This seems too subtle to me. Kyle would probably want to do something more obvious— something that would give him quick results."

"Just the same," I said, pushing my glasses up on my nose, "we'll investigate him. He might very well be our culprit."

"You're the private eyes," Jeff said. "Well, I'm going to go shower. I'll catch you guys later." He got up, grabbed his glove and ambled off to the locker room.

Ollie, Nina and I looked at each other and shrugged. This case seemed simple and straightforward, but I had a hunch it wasn't going to stay that way for long. I headed home to enter what we had found out about *The Case of the Stolen Signs* on my computer.

Δ   Δ   Δ

As we rode to the Muskrats' practice on Tuesday, Nina

suggested that we talk to her old neighbor, Frankie Dunbar.

"I used to play with his little sister when they lived on my block," Nina explained. "He moved about three years ago, when he was a freshman at Millhouse High School. Now he plays for the Muskrats, but he didn't play in yesterday's game. I guess he's just a sub."

"You think he'll be able to help us?" Ollie asked.

"I think so," Nina replied, and then seemed to change her mind. "Well, it's worth a try anyway."

The Muskrats were in the middle of batting practice when we arrived.

"That's Frankie," Nina informed us, pointing to the player jogging in from rightfield.

When the Muskrats started fielding practice, Frankie and a few others were sitting on the bench, waiting to be put in. Nina suggested that we talk to him right then, while he wasn't busy.

"Hi, Frankie," Nina said. "Remember me?"

"Hey, Nina!" he exclaimed, obviously very surprised to see her. "Wow, I haven't seen you since we moved. How are you?"

"I'm great. How about yourself?" Nina asked.

"Good," he replied, taking his glove off. "My little sister tells me you're part of some detective squad or something."

"Yeah, I am," Nina giggled at the coincidence. "The Jack B. Quick Detective Squad—and this is Jack B. Quick," she said, introducing me. "And," Nina said, pulling Ollie front and center, "this is Ollie Steele, our other associate."

"Glad to meet you, guys," he said, shaking our hands.

"It's funny that you mentioned the detective squad, Frankie," Nina said, putting on a more serious, businesslike face, "because we're here on business. You heard about the stolen signs?"

"Yeah, who hasn't?" he asked rhetorically. "It's all over the school."

"I can imagine," Nina said. "I was wondering, though, if you could help us out a little?"

"What do you mean, help you out?" Frankie asked, a little defensively.

"Maybe you have some information that could help our case," I cut in before Frankie thought Nina was accusing him. "Would you mind if we asked you some questions?"

"Go ahead," Frankie responded with a little more warmth.

"Well, to begin with," Nina said, flipping her long, jet-black braid over her shoulder, "do you have any idea who might be the culprit?"

"No, I really don't," Frankie replied after a moment.

"Well," I said, jumping into the questioning, "how about someone who would want the Muskrats to lose?" Frankie shook his head. "Can you think of any connections between the Muskrats, the Vikings and the Tigers?"

Again, Frankie shook his head. Then, suddenly, he sat straight up. "Yeah," he practically shouted. "Jon Polk!"

"What are you? Nuts?" Jeff asked Frankie. We had been so involved in questioning Frankie that none of us had even noticed when Jeff had jogged in to pick up a bat. "Jon wouldn't do something like this," Jeff continued.

"He might not do it all by himself," Frankie persisted, "but he has a cousin who plays on the Vikings and another on the Tigers. Who knows?"

"You mean that they might be conspiring to take the Muskrats down?" I asked Frankie.

"I guess it does seem a little ridiculous, but you never know," Frankie said with a sigh.

"That's right," I told Frankie. "You never know." I eyed him over the top of my glasses. It was nothing personal; I just like using my "detective look and attitude" on people when I meet them on a case. It helps them realize that even though we are only in junior high, we are definitely serious about this whole investigating thing.

"Hey, Dunbar!" Coach Branson called from the backstop. "Get out in rightfield. Hey, Josh, sit down for a while!" Joshua Edwards jogged in from rightfield. He was the regular rightfielder, but even benchwarmers like Frankie need to practice.

"Hey, Jeff," Ollie said. He had been rubbing his hair, which is cut in a high-top fade, during the whole conversation with Frankie. When Ollie does that, it means he is having a little trouble with something.

"Yeah, Ollie?" Jeff Robbins replied.

"What do you think about this Jon Polk triangle?" he asked. "Do you think it has any validity?"

"Not unless Jon's cousins are blackmailing him to give up the signs," he said, laughing a little, as if he thought the idea ludicrous. "Jon wouldn't sell out the team, no way. You should hear him brag about how good we are. He gets a big trip out of the fact that we've been champions for the past three years," Jeff explained. "This is his last year here. There's no way in the world he would give up a four-year string of championships."

"Maybe he is being blackmailed," I suggested. "Never rule out a possibility, Jeff."

"What are you saying about Jon?" asked Josh Edwards, the rightfielder, who had just taken a seat.

"Oh, nothing," Jeff answered Josh. "I was just saying how it's ridiculous to think that Jon Polk was the one who gave up the signs."

"Tell me about it!" Josh exclaimed. "Jon's the most die-hard Muskrat there is."

"By the way, Josh," Jeff said, "this is Jack, Nina and Ollie. They're trying to find out who's stealing our signs."

"Nice to meet you, Josh," I said, shaking his hand. "Do you have any idea who it might be?" I asked the rightfielder. He took off his hat, revealing a crew cut, and then wiped his forehead with a towel.

"Yeah, actually," he finally replied. "Kyle Sampson."

"They've been through that one, Josh," Jeff said.

"Do you know where we can find him?" I asked. "I think we should ask him a few questions."

"He works over at that gas station on the corner of Pacific and Pines Bridge," Jeff offered, "but I'm not sure if he's working today."

"Well, thanks," I told Josh and Jeff. "Let's go check out that gas station," I said, turning to my associates.

When we got there, we found out that Kyle wouldn't be working until the following afternoon.

Ollie and I returned to the Muskrats' practice without Nina because she had to babysit her little sister, Pam. When we arrived, it was nearly five o'clock, and the Muskrats were still in fielding practice. Frankie Dunbar and a few other players, the same ones I had noticed before, were sitting on the bench. I figured they must be the second string.

"Hi, Frankie," I called, approaching the bench.

"Hey, Jack. Hey, Ollie," he greeted us. "Where's Nina?"

"She went home," I explained. "Her mother's making her watch Pam."

"Oh, well, I would have liked to talk to her some more about our old neighborhood," he said. "Do you want to sit down?" Frankie asked, sliding over to make room for us.

"Thanks," Ollie said, plopping down. "Do you guys get to play much?" Ollie asked curiously.

"No, not really," Frank responded. "We're what you might call the benchwarmers."

"Oh," Ollie replied.

"Well, sometimes we're put in as pinch runners, or pinch hitters," Frankie explained.

"Well," Ollie said with a shrug, "I guess that's better than nothing."

"Yeah," Frankie sighed, "I suppose so." He leaned forward, resting his elbows on his knees and his chin on his hands.

"Hey, Jack," Frankie said a moment later, rotating his

head toward me. "You know, I've been thinking."

"About what, Frankie?" I asked, pushing my glasses up. Perhaps he had a new clue for the case.

"What if it isn't someone on the team?" he conjectured. "What if it's, like, someone's girlfriend or little brother or something?"

"It very well could be," I said. "However," I continued, "how would they know the signs? Would any of the players tell them to their girlfriends?"

"Sure!" he exclaimed. "Heck, I do it all the time. My girlfriend gets a kick out of it. In fact, last night I taught her the steal sign. It goes like this." He stood up, touched his cap, his left hip and then tugged on his right earlobe, all with his right hand. "That means steal a base," he explained.

Next, Frankie took off his cap and wiped his forehead with his left arm, while tugging on his belt buckle with his right. "That means bunt."

Then Frankie took his hat off with his left hand and tugged on his belt, while wiping his forehead with his right arm. He replaced his cap and tugged on his left ear with his left hand.

"That means take a pitch," Frankie said. "When Coach Branson sticks a pencil behind his left ear, it means swing for your life."

"Do you ever change the signs?" I asked Frankie.

"Yeah, these are the new signs," Frankie told me as if I were crazy to think otherwise. "We just changed them before the last game, and they've already been stolen."

"How often do you change them?" I asked.

"This was the only time," Frankie replied. "You see, we had over a week to memorize the new signs. That way, we wouldn't be on base and get the sign from the coach to steal, but forget what the sign meant."

"So, basically," I said, summarizing what Frankie was telling me, "the coach just changed the signs for the playoffs."

"Yeah," Frankie replied, leaning forward on his arms again.

"Yesterday's game was the first time you used these new signs?" Ollie asked.

"Yeah," he said in exasperation. "I couldn't believe it. You would think that if somebody had our signs, they would have the old ones, not the new ones."

"Perhaps," I said. "Does your girlfriend know these new signs?"

"I don't . . . " he began, but then his voice trailed off. "My girlfriend would never, ever do something like that. I can't believe you guys would even suggest it!"

"You suggested it!" Ollie exclaimed. "It was your idea that a player's girlfriend might be stealing your signs, not ours."

"Oh, yeah," Frankie replied. "Hey, you know, something else just occurred to me."

"Oh, really? What's that?" Ollie asked sarcastically— like a cop questioning a lying suspect.

"Do you remember, Jack," Frankie said, ignoring Ollie, "when you asked about a connection between the Muskrats, the Vikings and the Tigers?"

"Yes, I do," I replied, knitting my eyebrows. "You mentioned Jon Polk."

"Well, I was just thinking," Frankie said, sitting back and removing his cap. "Coach Branson's business rival, Gene Riley, is the coach of the Roosevelt Tigers."

"Business rival?" Ollie asked. "I thought the coach was a teacher of some sort."

"Well, he is," Frankie said. "He's a substitute teacher. But Coach Branson and Coach Riley have been in business since they were in the minor leagues. That's how they know each other," he explained. "They started a real estate company together."

"They own a company together?" Ollie asked. "How can they be rivals then?" Good point, Ol, I thought.

"Well, now they each have their own companies," Frankie explained.

"O.K., guys," Coach Branson's booming voice interrupted our conversation. "Line up for sprints."

"Oh, I've got to run," Frankie sighed, getting up and donning his cap. "Literally. I hate sprints."

"See you later," I called after him. Frankie trotted off to home plate, where the team was lining up for sprints to first.

Ollie agreed to meet me at my house after dinner. I told him I'd ask Nina to come over, too.

Ollie showed up at around seven and we went upstairs to my room to enter the new info into my computer. I really don't understand what people did before computers.

"Hi, guys," Nina greeted us about 10 minutes later.

Ollie and I were sitting under the lamp I have over my computer. It's the only light I keep on in my room when I'm working. It helps me focus my thoughts.

"How did it go after I left you this afternoon?" Nina asked, taking a seat.

"Well, we talked to Frankie some more," I explained, spinning my chair to face her. "He came up with an interesting connection."

I spun back and started to enter the new data into my computer as I explained to Nina.

"But first," I said, typing away, "he mentioned the Jon Polk triangle involving his cousins. You were there for that, remember?" I glanced over to my bed and saw her nodding in the dim light.

"Well," I went on, turning back to the computer. "When we returned, he also told us that Roosevelt's coach, Gene Riley, is Coach Branson's business rival."

"Interesting," Nina said. "Have you talked to Coach Branson yet?"

"No," Ollie replied. "We should do that tomorrow. And we can't forget to talk to Kyle Sampson, either."

"Quite right," I agreed, "but right now I should study. I have a math quiz tomorrow."

"O.K.," Nina said, standing up. "Let's go, Ollie. You know how Jack is when he has to study!"

"Yeah," Ollie said, laughing.

I felt a little insulted. I didn't think I was *that* bad.

Δ   Δ   Δ

The next day, after school, Nina and Ollie went to

interview Kyle, and I made my way to Millhouse High. I wanted to talk to the coach before the Muskrats started their practice. I told Nina and Ollie to meet me there after they had talked to Kyle.

"Hi, Mr. Branson," I greeted him, as he approached the field from the parking lot.

"Good afternoon, Jack," he said smiling. "Any news?"

"Well, my associates are questioning Kyle right now," I explained, "but I'm here because I wanted to talk to you."

"About what?" he asked. I walked over and joined him in the dugout.

"About Gene Riley," I stated.

"Gene?" he asked, obviously puzzled. "What about him?"

"He's the coach of the Tigers and your competition in the local real estate business, correct?" I asked.

"Correct," he replied, a little puzzled, as if he couldn't tell where I was headed.

"In the past two of your last three championships," I said, wiping my lenses on my T-shirt, "you played and beat the Tigers."

"Yeah," the coach admitted, "but I've known Gene since the minors and we've always been rivals when our teams played each other—friendly rivals.

"Like last year," he kept on explaining, "when we went out for a beer after the last game, Gene said to me, 'Buddy, next year I'm going to beat you.' He looked me square in the eye and said again, 'One way or another, I'm going to beat you.' "

"Doesn't sound too friendly to me," I offered.

"Well, it was," Coach Branson assured me. "He wouldn't go stealing my signs. He may even use the same ones that I do, for all I know."

"Didn't you just change your signs?" I asked.

"Yeah, but they're the same ones I always use," Buddy Branson explained. "I just change what they stand for."

"So even if Coach Riley recognized them," I continued, "he wouldn't know what you were telling your players, right?"

"Right," Mr. Branson replied. "He couldn't know unless someone told him."

"Somebody probably will—just as they did when you played Central," I informed him. "Well, we'll be here tomorrow, investigating the game."

"O.K., Jack," he said, getting up from the bench. "Good luck with the investigation."

"Thanks," I said. "Good luck in tomorrow's game."

"I may need it," he said, and went to round up his team.

Ollie and Nina appeared just then, and they plopped down next to me on the bench.

"So what did Kyle have to say?" I asked them both.

"Actually," Nina began, "he seemed kind of reluctant to say anything."

"Oh, really?" I said, sitting up straight. Nina had my full attention, now that it sounded as if Kyle was a legitimate suspect.

"Yeah," Ollie continued, taking the reins. "He admitted he was kicked off the team, and that he was mad at the coach and all. But he kind of over-emphasized that he didn't even remember what the signs were—you know what I mean?"

"Yeah," I said. "Go on."

"Well," Nina jumped in, "he also pointed out that if the signs had been changed, then the signs that he knew were wrong."

"Right," I agreed.

"But," Nina said, "that was all he would tell us. He gave us no other information—not even to push the blame away from himself."

"Well," I said, leading the way to the bicycles, "we should show up early tomorrow. The game starts at four, but I want to be here by three o'clock, which is only fifteen minutes after school ends. Do you think we can make it in fifteen minutes?"

"We can if we hurry," Ollie answered.

"Then we'll hurry!" I told them both.

Δ   Δ   Δ

Once that school bell rang at 2:45 on Thursday, I was on my bike like a shot, as were Nina and Ollie. We got there before three o'clock, surprisingly, and the teams weren't even on the field yet. However, we arrived just as Coach Branson came storming into the dugout where we were sitting. I half expected to see smoke coming out of his ears. He threw his briefcase on the bench.

"What's wrong, Coach?" I asked calmly.

"Gene stole my briefcase last night!" he practically screamed.

"Then what's that?" Ollie wanted to know, pointing to

the case the coach had thrown on the bench.

"That's Gene's!" he yelled. His cheeks were flaming red, and his forehead was glistening with sweat.

"My combinations don't work on the lock," he said, toning down his anger. "I tried about a hundred times. We have identical briefcases," he explained.

"How could he get your briefcase if you don't work in the same office?" I asked.

"Last night there was a real estate brokers' conference," Buddy Branson explained. "We always sit next to each other, but this time he snatched my briefcase."

"Maybe it was an honest mistake," I offered as an explanation. "After all, you have the same briefcases."

"But does his have the team roster, batting lineup, team stats and a list of signs in it?" he retorted disgustedly. "I can't believe I left everything in it!"

"Everything was in your briefcase?" Ollie asked him with an astonished expression.

"Everything," the coach repeated, kicking the dirt with his shoe. "I'll be back. I have to change into my uniform," he said, walking off to the locker room and his office.

I examined the briefcase and recognized it as the same kind, or one, that Coach Branson had been carrying on Monday. Then I checked for initials, and found the letters G.S.R. printed next to the handle.

"Well," I told my squad, "this is Gene Riley's all right. His initials are on it."

We waited there in silence, relaxing in the shade of the dugout. After a few minutes, the coach returned unchanged, dragging Kyle by his collar. Neither of them looked happy.

"He was stealing this," Coach Branson said, tossing a bag at our feet. When it hit the ground, baseballs spilled all around the dugout. "Sit down!" he ordered Kyle, who promptly sat on the end of the bench.

We stood up and joined the coach.

"What happened?" Ollie asked.

"When I went to change," Coach Branson explained, "I used the field entrance to the locker room, as usual. When I walked in the door, Kyle bumped into me on his way out. Evidently, he was attempting to relieve the team of its baseballs."

"Look," Kyle blurted out, "I just wanted to get even, all right? I'm still not too happy that you kicked me off the team, you know!"

"Maybe if you had showed me that you have what it takes to be a team player," the coach suggested, "I wouldn't have let you go. You're a good ballplayer, Kyle, but you don't play for the team. If you want to compete for yourself, take up running or something." He paused and then went on. "I'm willing to let you play, if you're willing to put the team first. You have one more year of high school, so you can try out again next year. You're good enough to make it, but are you good enough to stay on the team?"

"You mean all I have to do is be a team ballplayer and I'll be set?" Kyle asked, his blue eyes wide with shock at the simplicity of it.

"Well, not exactly," the coach said, "but that's a lot of it. First, you have to serve detention for stealing the balls.

Second, you have to prove to me and to the team that you really can be a team ballplayer."

"That doesn't sound so bad," Kyle admitted. "I've served detention before, I can do it again."

"By the way," I said to Kyle. "How did you learn the new signs? They were just changed over vacation last week."

"I don't know the signs," he claimed. "I'm not the guy you're all looking for. I don't know who is. Like I said, I just wanted to get even," he confessed.

No one said anything for a full minute. "Do you think I would have pulled this if I was giving the signs to the other teams?" Kyle demanded.

"No, I suppose not," Coach Branson said.

"You mean you're going to take his word for it?" Ollie asked, exasperated.

"Yes, Ollie," Coach replied. "I believe him. Kyle, you want to stay and watch the game anyway? I'll let you sit in the dugout."

Kyle grinned. "Sure, Coach, I'd love to. And I'm real sorry about what I did—all season. I sure learned my lesson."

A few minutes later, after Kyle had left, Coach Branson turned to me and said, "Then it has to be Gene."

"Buddy! Hey, Buddy!" a man suddenly called from across the field. He was carrying a briefcase just like Coach Branson's.

"I got your briefcase, Bud," he yelled, holding it up. He walked over and descended into the dugout. "I realized it when I got home. I went to pull out some papers, but my combos didn't work, then I saw your initials on it. You have mine?"

"Uh, yeah," Coach replied, a little meekly. "It's right here," he said, grabbing it off of the bench.

"Oh, good," Coach Riley sighed. "You couldn't get into it, could you?"

"No, why?" Coach Branson asked.

"I have my sign list, team stats, lineups and everything in there," Coach Riley explained.

"Funny," Coach Branson said, "so do I." The two exchanged briefcases and shook hands. "Good luck."

"Same to you, Buddy," Gene said, and walked over to his own dugout.

Another suspect knocked out of the running, I thought.

When the game was about to start, I positioned Nina by the Tigers' dugout, Ollie by the Muskrats' dugout and myself with the spectators in the bleachers. The stands were packed with Millhouse locals who had come to cheer for the Muskrats.

Don Frazer was pitching for the Muskrats that afternoon. He is no Jeff Robbins, but he can hold his own. He struck out the first three batters.

To start the game for the Muskrats, Mike Moore, the catcher, and Preston Bates, the shortstop, struck out and flew out, respectively, in the bottom of the first. Jon Polk got the first hit of the game. He singled to center on a count of one ball and two strikes.

While Jon was on first, I noticed him making idle

conversation with the Tiger first baseman. Next up was Tommy Petrosino, the centerfielder, and he was thrown out at first after a grounder to short.

Jon then made his way over to third base and waited for one of his teammates to bring his glove out to him. Then the Tiger first baseman, the one Jon had been chatting with, came over to talk with Jon again.

At this point, I guessed that the first baseman must be Jon's cousin whom Frankie had mentioned before. Then I noticed Jon whisper something in his cousin's ear while apparently trying to conceal a small piece of paper he was slipping to him at the same time. All those boasts about Jon's loyalty to the Muskrats seemed to be empty now.

When Jon's cousin walked into his dugout, Nina came scrambling across the field and bumped into him. I thought she was crazy to run across the field in the middle of the game. I watched as she talked, presumably apologizing for being so clumsy. Then she scurried the rest of the way across the field to Ollie.

During the top of the second inning, Ollie and Nina came up to my seat. Nina handed me a piece of paper.

"What's this?" I asked, although I suspected that I already knew.

"It's the note that Jon passed to his cousin on the field," Nina replied smugly. "I took it out of his pocket when I ran into him."

"I'm impressed!" I exclaimed, looking at Nina admiringly. Sometimes, my associates truly amaze me. I unfolded the note, read it over and started to laugh. When I read it aloud to them, Nina and Ollie began to laugh too.

Dear Marty,
I'm only doing this because you're my cousin, but
here's Joanna's number: 795-5934. You owe me one!
                                        Jon

"Well," I said, catching my breath. "So much for our Jon Polk triangle theory."

"I can't believe I stole that note from him!" Nina exclaimed, her dark eyes wide in surprise.

"Yeah," Ollie laughed. "That was pretty classy. You'd make a great pickpocket!"

"Anyway," I said, interrupting my associates, "we've pretty much ruled out all of our suspects now."

"Let's watch the game anyway," Nina suggested. "Just to see if the signs are still being stolen."

Indeed they were. It was like a tragic rerun of the Muskrats' game against the Vikings—except that this time the Muskrats lost. The Tigers beat them 6-1. Now the Muskrats had to win the remaining two games of the series to take the championship, and it would obviously be tough with their signs being stolen.

At the end of the ninth, my squad and I discussed a few ideas and then went down to the bench to talk with Coach Branson.

"Any ideas, kids?" he asked, as we walked down the few steps to the dugout.

"No, sir," I replied. "However, we do have a suggestion

to make, if both you and Coach Riley agree."

"What's that?" Coach Branson asked.

"My father owns a video camera," Nina explained, "and we were wondering if we could videotape tomorrow's game?"

"I don't see why not," Coach Branson said, shrugging his massive shoulders. "Hey, Gene," he yelled across the infield to the Tigers' dugout.

Gene Riley hopped out of the dugout and came over to Buddy Branson. After he heard what we had to say, he agreed to the taping, saying that he hoped we were good with a camera. Nina then went to Jon's cousin in the Tigers' dugout and returned the slip of paper and apologized again for bumping into him.

I headed home about 15 minutes later, wondering how we could have lost all our suspects in the space of a few hours.

Δ　　Δ　　Δ

We arrived at the ballfield a little bit later on Friday than we had on Thursday because we had to go to Nina's and pick up the video equipment first.

Nina didn't set up the camera on a stationary stand because she wanted to move around. Besides, it made it easier for us to videotape what we wanted to, and not just the game. We had told the coaches that we were taping the game, but what we really wanted was to tape the dugouts, the players and all the coaches, including the ones at first and third bases.

After the game began, it became clear that the signs

were being stolen yet again. Coach Branson hadn't changed all of them after the game the day before because it would have been too confusing for his players. Instead, he had come up with another plan. He was telling players what to do before they got on the field. Using this strategy, the Muskrats were able to play ball to their usual high standard. However, I noticed that the few plays that Coach Branson signaled openly ended in outs. Still, the Muskrats won 5-4 off a Jon Polk homer. Stolen signs don't mean anything when a ball lands over the fence.

Nina, Ollie and I took the tape we had made back to Nina's place that night and reviewed it. Sure enough, we found what we had been looking for. It wasn't pure proof, but tomorrow's game would show whether it was good enough.

I immediately got on the phone and called Coach Branson. He invited us all to come to his house with the tape and show him what we had.

"Well," Coach Branson said with a sigh after viewing the tape. "What do you suggest I do? I can't change the signs. No one will know what to do—it'll be too confusing."

I thought for a moment, and then an idea popped into my head. They usually do.

"I think you should rotate some of the signs," I explained. "Just tell the starters—not the benchwarmers."

"That shouldn't be too hard," Coach Branson said, catching onto my scheme. "The subs will never know."

Δ   Δ   Δ

The last game of the series was played at Roosevelt

High because the first two had been at Millhouse. The Tigers, as the home team, took the field first. There weren't as many Muskrat fans at Roosevelt, but I did recognize quite a few from the first two games.

It was a long game—it went 10 innings. I thought it was obvious after the first few innings that the Tigers were trying to get an advantage from the Muskrat signs—but it didn't work this time. The Muskrats proved victorious, winning 1-0, and were champions for the fourth year in a row!

However, it wasn't all over yet. My squad and I went to Coach Branson, who in turn summoned our culprit.

"What are you talking about?" Frankie asked, when I had laid it all out for him.

"Look," I began to explain calmly, "we have a videotape of you using hand signals to give the Muskrats' signs to the Tigers."

"But—" Frankie began to protest, but Coach Branson interrupted him.

"I saw the tape myself, Frankie," he said solemnly. "Why? Why did you do it?"

Frankie's eyes were wide with disbelief, but he finally realized that he had been caught. He slumped down on the bench and rested his chin on his chest.

"I figured that if we lost, you would make some changes in the lineup," Frankie admitted. "I want to start. I'm sick of scouting my own team for weaknesses, although it gave me the greatest chance to steal the signs."

"Why did you think you would start if we were losing?" Coach Branson asked. "You must have realized I would probably keep you on the bench—especially after the first game."

"Yeah," Frankie responded. "That's why I kept doing it. I guess you could call it revenge."

We were all quiet for a moment. It was an awkward silence that I wanted to break, but I didn't know what to say.

"By the way," Frankie spoke up, rescuing me, "that was pretty clever of you to rotate the signs again," he said, looking at the coach. "I didn't realize that was what you had done, and by the time I discovered it, it was too late in the game. I knew you had changed them, but I didn't know how."

"Who would have thought you and Kyle would be so upset with the situation?" Buddy Branson mused to himself. "Next year you'll have a good chance," he explained to Frankie. "I think you should serve some detention with Kyle and talk it over. Maybe I'll have you do a little community service with the Little League, too. I had a few plans for the both of you, actually. You have what it takes, just like Kyle, but I have to play the seniors, too, and this season they were good enough to stay in. Next year, you'll be in the same position."

"The others are wrong too, Coach Branson," I added. "Whoever was accepting Frankie's signals is wrong. I think you should have a talk with Gene Riley and the Viking coach about that."

"Good idea, Jack," he agreed. "Sportsmanship goes down the tubes when this happens, and that takes the fun out of sports. Everyone loses in the end."

"Hey, Jack," Nina said. "Don't you have anything else to say?"

I smiled and said the most satisfying two words that I know, "Case closed."

The Case
of the
Foiled
Fencers

"Wow! There's so much going on at once!" Nina exclaimed as the two of us took our seats in the gymnasium stands at Fieldview High School.

Nina and I were just in time to catch the tail end of the regional qualifying round for the state high school fencing finals, a two-day competition. The first day of the finals, it was also the first time either Nina or I had ever seen fencing in person. Oh, sure, I'd seen sword fights in movies like *Robin Hood* and *The Princess Bride*, but this was different— this was real competitive fencing.

"Where's Ollie?" Nina wondered, flipping her black braid over her shoulder and scanning the gym. Nina and Ollie are members of the Jack B. Quick Detective Squad and are invaluable associates. I'm Jack, by the way, and solving sports crimes is my game. We weren't there on a case, though. We were just spectators.

"I don't know where he is, but he'd better hurry," I

replied. I found it strange that Ollie was so late. He's not a punctual kind of guy, but his friend and one-time babysitter, Joe Repa, was competing for Fieldview High in a few minutes. I knew that Ollie did not want to miss that match.

Central High had already clinched third place, leaving Roosevelt and Fieldview to battle it out for first. Nina and I watched as Mike Dougall of Fieldview set up for his match against his Roosevelt opponent, John Brady. Mike was standing on the fencing strip that ran parallel to the bleachers where we were sitting. The strip is regulation size: 15 yards long and 1 yard wide. From the reading I had done, I knew that the strips where the fencers do combat are often made of copper, so that they will be grounded. This is important because fencers' touches are registered electrically.

Mike and John were both dressed in standard fencing uniforms—white close-fitting knickers and jackets, with protective wire-mesh masks over their faces. When they were ready, the director (or fencing judge) called out the start command, "Fence!"

Mike lunged with his sword, which was about a yard long and called an epée [*eh-PAY*], forcing John to retreat out of the sword's reach. Mike kept advancing. Then, when he lunged again, so did John. They both touched each other with the tips of their weapons. At that moment the red and green lights on the scoring machine lit up. The machine is a little larger than a shoe box and it was positioned on a table by the side of the strip.

"Halt!" the director called. Both Mike and John stopped in their tracks.

"What is going on, Jack?" Nina asked, wrinkling her forehead in confusion. "They just started. Why are they stopping already?"

"They've both scored a hit," I replied with a small smile. "The score is now 1-1." I never gloat as a rule, but I love knowing something Nina doesn't once in a while. It doesn't happen very often.

She glared at me, so I wiped the smile off my face and explained to her what I understood to be the basics of scoring. Each fencer is connected to the scoring machine by a wire that runs through a reel. The reel keeps the wire out of the fencer's way and is located at his end of the strip. This wire is then connected to the fencer's body cord, which fits beneath his clothes and then runs out of his sleeve, where it is attached to his sword. I made a mental note to ask Ollie whether the wire was part of the fencer's equipment or part of the machine.

"Fence!" the director boomed again. This time John attacked first, but Mike was ready for him. He parried (that means he blocked John's sword with his own) and then lunged for a touch.

"Halt!" the director called once again. Mike was now ahead 2-1 in the five-minute bout. When the action started again, another double touch was registered, bringing the score to 3-2 in Mike's favor.

Then John took control of the strip. He advanced on Mike, who retreated as far as he could go. I knew that if Mike stepped off the strip, John would get a point, but Mike attacked to save himself. However, John was ready for him, and counter-attacked, earning a point and tying the score. The command to fence was barely out of the director's mouth when John attacked again, scoring the go-ahead point with his touch. The score was now 4-3 in John's favor.

"How do they decide the winner?" Nina asked.

"It's the first fencer to get five points," I replied. "John needs just one more point to take the match."

"Fence!" the director called again. Mike and John lunged and parried with each other for several seconds, and then Mike made his move, lunging low when John expected him to go high. He made the touch and the score was tied at 4-4. The next touch would win the bout.

"Fence!" the director commanded again. Blades clashed together as Mike and John advanced and retreated along the strip. Both fencers were looking for any weakness in the other that might lead to an opening—and the win. Then an odd thing happened. Mike began to retreat. Naturally, John advanced on him. But it was a trick! Suddenly, Mike started his own advance with more determination in his thrusts and parries than we had seen up until that moment. Mike made one last thrust, touched John's shoulder with his epée, and scored the winning point. It was too late for John. Mike had won. Cheers rose from the Fieldview fans as the two fencers shook hands.

"That was incredible!" Nina exclaimed. "I love this sport. Think we can get them to start a fencing team at Johnson?"

"I don't know," I replied. "But it's worth a try."

"There he is!" Nina exclaimed suddenly. "Ollie! Over

here!" Nina yelled, standing up and waving wildly to get Ollie's attention. That's one thing about Nina. She can sure make her voice carry in a crowd.

"Phew, I made it," Ollie said, plopping himself down next to us on the bleachers. "How's Fieldview doing?"

"Well, if Joe wins, then Fieldview's going to the state finals," Nina told Ollie with a grin.

"Way to go!" Ollie exclaimed. "Hey, have you guys had any trouble following the action?"

"Not really," I replied. Ollie is our fencing expert. Since Joe had babysat for him a lot when he was younger, Ollie had learned a great deal about the sport. Joe is one of Ollie's idols. "Hey, Ol, I do have one question," I continued. "Is the body cord that connects the fencer to the scoring machine wire part of the fencer's equipment or is it part of the machinery?"

"I'm almost positive the body cord belongs to the fencer," Ollie answered. "The machinery is standardized, so there's never a problem with wires not working with different machines. It's kind of like how your computer at home is compatible with the ones at school."

We watched as Alan Flynn of Roosevelt High and Joe Repa hooked their body cords to the scoring machine wires at a strip on the far side of the gym. I noticed that there were eight fencing strips positioned around the gym in groups of two.

"Hey, Ol," Nina began, blowing a small bubble with her pink bubble gum. "Does it hurt when they get stabbed?"

"No, the swords aren't sharp," Ollie replied. "Actually,

they have flat buttons at the tips that depress when pressed against a target. They're not made for fencing to the death, or anything like that."

"Not like a Samurai sword, huh?" I said. I had recently seen this Japanese horror movie in which this guy has to stab a bunch of other guys in order to defend the honor of his family. As a rule I don't go in for horror, but there had been something about this movie that made me watch it through till the end.

"Anyway, in fencing, when the round piece is pressed against an opponent, it sends a signal through the wire to the scoring machine and that causes the light to go on," Ollie continued, ignoring my comment.

"Which one is Joe?" Nina interrupted, looking from one masked fencer to the other.

"He's on the right," Ollie said. "Whenever he scores a touch, the green light will go on. When Alan scores, the red light will go on."

"And when both lights go on, it's a double touch. That's when both fencers score touches at the same time," I added.

"You got it, Jack," Ollie confirmed. "Hey, they're about to start."

Joe and Alan clashed their blades, but Alan released quickly and scored the first touch.

"Come on, Joe!" Ollie yelled. "You can do it!"

Joe and Alan started fencing again at the director's command, each battling for the next touch. Finally, they both lunged forward, scoring what seemed to be a double touch— except that Joe's light did not go on! A touch was awarded to Alan, bringing the score in the bout to 2-0.

"No way!" a Fieldview fan shouted. "Get a new director!"

"Looks like there's something wrong with the equipment," I said to Ollie.

"Hmm," Ollie replied. "When I came into the gym I heard that there had been some equipment problems."

"Oh, yeah?" I asked, my interest piqued. Something was beginning to smell a little fishy.

"Yeah, I heard that three or four fencers had trouble with their connections," Ollie said, trying to keep his attention focused on the action in front of him.

The director took a timeout and allowed Joe to check his sword. Sure enough, it wasn't working properly—neither were his two extra epées. Following regulations, the director gave Joe a warning because every fencer is personally responsible for maintaining his equipment.

"That is totally unlike Joe," Ollie commented with a frown. "He would never let his equipment go to pieces like that."

"Maybe we should talk to him after the bout," Nina suggested.

"You read my mind, Ms. Chin," I said. "Something unusual may be going on here. Let's head down to the Fieldview bench."

As Ollie, Nina and I made our way down through the bleachers, we could see Joe replacing his body cord. After he had finished, he stepped back onto the strip and hooked himself back up to the machine. Unfortunately, this cord did not work either. Before we had even made it to the bench, the director had disqualified Joe from the match. Fieldview had to put in a substitute fencer.

"No way!" exclaimed Ollie, his brown eyes flashing. "This is so unfair. Joe's season is over. He's been training so hard for so long. Those recruiters from Camden College will never be interested in him now."

"Recruiters?" I asked.

"Yeah," Ollie answered. "Camden has been interested in Joe for a while, but this was the first time they were actually going to see him fence. Plus, Camden only happens to be the best fencing college in the state."

"Hi, Joe," Ollie greeted his former babysitter as the three of us approached the bench. "Are you O.K.?"

"Yeah, I'm all right," Joe replied. "But I'm really teed-off. I don't understand how this could happen. I mean, none of my equipment works."

"Do you remember my friends Jack B. Quick and Nina Chin?" Ollie asked, motioning to us.

"Sure, I do," Joe replied, looking up from putting his equipment away. "Hi, guys."

"I'm sorry about what happened, Joe," I said.

"Thanks," he said slowly. "The worst part is that the team has no chance of winning the title now, and it's all my fault."

"Joseph!" an adult voice behind us called. We all turned to see Bill Magnuson, the county athletic commissioner and a member of the Bout Committee, walking toward the bench. "I just heard, Joseph, and I'm sorry. I hope you understand that the director had no choice in the matter."

"I know, sir," Joe said glumly.

"Hello, Mr. Magnuson," I greeted him. I know Mr. Magnuson fairly well since a number of our investigations have involved him in one way or another.

"Hello, Jack," Mr. Magnuson replied. I noticed that the top of his bald head was glistening the way it usually does when he's agitated. "And Ollie and Nina, too. I'm glad the three of you are here."

"Why's that, Mr. Magnuson?" I asked.

"Well, we may need your services, Jack," the commissioner said. "I've had a chance to review the records of today's events, and I'm extremely concerned. Look at this, Joe," he finished, handing him a computer printout. "Notice anything unusual?"

Joe ran his finger down the page. "Seven disqualifications?" he finally said.

"And twenty warnings for equipment failures," the commissioner pointed out. "This is unprecedented! I've spoken with the directors, and we all agree that no one has ever seen so many equipment malfunctions in one tournament."

Joe handed me the sheet of paper, his blue eyes full of concern.

"Which is where you come in, Jack," Mr. Magnuson said, clearing his throat. "I want you and your squad to get to the bottom of this."

I scanned the list quickly before handing it to Ollie and Nina. "What exactly do you want us to do?"

"Well, the odds of this many malfunctions happening by chance are close to nil. I think something went wrong. Or, more precisely," he paused, looking each of us in the eye in turn, "some*one* went wrong."

"You mean you think someone has been messing with our equipment?" Joe asked, a shocked expression on his face.

"I'm convinced," the commissioner replied firmly. "I'm going to suggest that the Bout Committee ask Jack and his detective squad to investigate the matter. Meet me at their table in about 15 minutes, O.K., Jack?" After patting Joe quickly on the shoulder, the commissioner walked away across the gym floor.

Just then, the last match finished. Since it was the final match of the day, the Bout Committee had moved the fencers to the strip right in front of the bleachers. Tim Burns, Joe's substitute, lost to Alan, 5-1. Joe looked more depressed than before at this turn of events. He was so overwhelmed, in fact, that he didn't notice when his teammate Mike Dougall started to smile. Mike was the only guy on the Fieldview bench with a grin on his face. I thought it was kind of weird, even though Mike had won his own match earlier against Roosevelt.

I knew Joe was upset, but I didn't want to waste this prime opportunity to question him. Call me cold-hearted, but a detective's got to do what he's got to do. "When was the last time before today's match that you fenced?" I inquired.

"Yesterday at practice," Joe replied.

"And all of your equipment was working fine then?" Nina asked quickly, beating me to my next question. As I have said before, Nina has a mind like a steel trap.

"Yes, it was working fine," Joe said. "I even re-tested everything after practice and there was nothing wrong. And then this morning I checked everything over again."

Just then, Alan Flynn, Roosevelt's top fencer, walked over to the Fieldview bench. Tall and slim, he has long brown hair that he had pulled back in a ponytail. "Sorry about your disqualification, Joe," he said. "You must be pretty steamed."

"You bet I am," Joe answered. "Especially now that I know someone may have messed with my equipment and a lot of other fencers' equipment on purpose. My friends here are on the case," he concluded, tilting his head in our direction.

Alan shot us a nervous glance. Nervous glances are a big help in my business. People give stuff away all the time with small gestures and little looks.

"Maybe we can fence again after tomorrow's competition," Alan suggested. "I still want to find out which one of us is really the best." With that, he turned and walked away.

"Hey, it's time to check with Mr. Magnuson," Nina exclaimed, looking at her watch.

"You know what, Nina?" I suggested in my take-charge detective voice. "You should probably stick with Joe for a while in case he thinks of anything important. Plus, you may see or hear something important if you hang out here."

Nina nodded her agreement. Actually, I think Nina

sometimes prefers working alone. She loves to try and beat me out to the solution to a case. So far, that's only happened once. But she was the culprit so I'm not sure if that really counts. That, as they say, is another story.

As soon as Mr. Magnuson saw Ollie and me coming, he waved us over. "You're on the case," the commissioner announced with a smile.

"When are you going to announce the official results of today's bouts, sir?" I asked immediately. I knew that we would need as much time as possible to conduct the investigation.

Mr. Magnuson cleared his throat. His head was really shining now. "The committee has decided to give you until seven o'clock tonight to solve this mystery. Otherwise, we'll have to go with the results as they stand now. I'm sorry, Jack, but it's the best I can do."

Seven o'clock, I thought, glancing down at my watch in dismay. That was less than two hours away—less than two hours to solve *The Case of the Foiled Fencers*. "O.K., Mr. Magnuson," I said. "We're on the case."

As soon as Ollie and I found Nina, I called a meeting in a corner of the gym. We reviewed what we had learned so far.

"Did Joe know of anyone who might want to hurt his chances of making it to the individuals tomorrow?" I asked Nina.

"No, but I did find out about some other fencers who might have had motives," she replied.

"Who?" Ollie wanted to know.

"Well, there's Joe's teammate on the Fieldview squad, Mike Dougall, for starters," Nina said.

"What would his motive be?" I asked, pushing my glasses up farther on my nose and staring at Nina.

"I know," Ollie interrupted. "Mike used to lose to Joe all the time in practice bouts. With Joe out of the way, Mike may have a chance of going to the state championship. A slim chance, but a chance all the same."

"Hey," I said suddenly. "Remember when Tim Burns, the guy who substituted for Joe in that last bout, lost? Well, I happened to be watching Mike Dougall at the time and he actually smiled as Tim's match ended."

"So much for team spirit!" Nina exclaimed.

"Anyone else, Nina?" I continued.

"Of course, there's the most obvious suspect—Alan Flynn," Nina answered.

"Alan and Joe have been rivals for a long time," Ollie agreed. "They just about split all of their bouts through high school." Ollie thought for a minute, running his hand across his high-top fade haircut. "I doubt Alan would have had anything to do with it, though. I mean, he's a pretty cocky guy. I'm sure he figures he'll beat Joe under any circumstances."

"O.K.," I agreed. "Then how do you explain the guilty look that crossed Alan's face when Joe told him we were investigating today's competition?"

"Good question," Ollie said with a shrug.

"I saw that look, too," Nina put in. "He's definitely hiding something. But don't forget John Brady, Alan's best friend on the Fieldview squad. I heard he's not a very good sport. Joe told me he has played some pretty nasty tricks in the past. One time, he actually broke one of his opponent's swords after a bout. He never got caught or anything, but everyone knew it was him."

"O.K., let's summarize," I said in an attempt to get my associates to focus. "Right now we have three suspects: Mike Dougall of Fieldview—his motive, revenge; Alan Flynn of Roosevelt—his motive, to make it to the fencing finals at any cost—"

"But he still wants to fence Joe one last time to prove to himself that he's the better fencer," Ollie cut in.

"Right," I agreed. "Finally, there's John Brady, the troublemaker, who may very well want to make sure that his best friend wins the trophy," I concluded.

"It looks like we have a massive equipment destroyer on our hands, Jack," Ollie pointed out. Sometimes Ollie is a master at stating the obvious. I just nodded absently. That wasn't all it looked like, though. Something had been nagging me about the day's results. Suddenly, it occurred to me what it was.

"We need to talk to Joe again," I said, motioning for Ollie and Nina to follow me.

Δ   Δ   Δ

"Joe, can you answer a few more questions for us?" I asked, as we stopped him on his way to the locker room.

"Shoot," he replied.

"Well, there are six other fencers who were disqualified," I began, showing him the printout. "Twenty others were given warnings for faulty equipment. I think that if we can find out what happened today then you and everyone else on the 'hit' list will be back in the competition."

"That would be great, guys," Joe said, "especially if I can convince those college scouts to stick around for a rematch." He looked over his shoulder toward the bleachers. I followed his gaze and saw four men wearing navy blue suits and brown shoes sitting in the almost empty stands, holding clipboards. In those uniforms, they were either FBI agents or scouts.

"College scouts," I repeated. "Are they only here to see you?"

"No way," Joe replied. "These competitions are a great way for the scouts to see all the local talent at once. I would guess that Alan, Mike and I are all on their list of fencers to watch."

"What about John Brady?" I asked casually.

"Maybe, but he's already been recruited," Joe explained. "I forget which college. My disqualification blows my chance of earning a scholarship to Camden, though. I could have used it, too."

"And Alan?" I continued.

"Well, since Roosevelt won today and I'm out of the competition, Alan's looking really good to them. He'll probably win the individuals tomorrow. If he does, he'll definitely get the scouts' attention," Joe answered. "I'd say it's a safe bet that he'll be offered a Camden scholarship."

We reassured Joe as best we could and then went off to

find the notorious Alan Flynn. Before I had even explained the situation to him, he cut me off.

"Yeah," he interrupted smugly, "without Joe in my way, I'll get into Camden, no problem."

Nina and Ollie looked at me. That was a pretty brash statement to make to three detectives.

"Don't get me wrong," Alan continued, with a toss of his ponytail, "I feel bad for Joe. It was rotten luck."

"Well, it appears that six other fencers had the same rotten luck," Ollie commented smoothly. He told Alan about the extraordinarily high number of disqualifications and warnings.

"Are you serious?" Alan responded in surprise.

"Quite serious," I said. "Here are the unofficial results of today's competition." I handed Alan the printout. His mouth dropped open—literally—as he scanned the list.

"This is unbelievable," Alan remarked. "This sort of thing never happens."

"It happened today," Nina said firmly. "What we want to know is who tampered with these fencers' equipment. Sabotage is the only possible explanation for so many errors."

"You don't think that *I* had anything to do with this?" Alan asked in disbelief.

"At this point, almost everyone is a suspect," I cut in smoothly. Nina has this habit of being so blunt that she sometimes scares people. "Let me ask you this," I continued. "Can you think of a reason why anyone would want to see all seven of these fencers disqualified?"

Alan looked at the list again. "No, I can't think of one. Plus, I don't even know some of these fencers." He thought for a second. "Hey, let me ask you guys something."

"Go ahead," I replied.

"It sounds like you're assuming that someone did a number on the equipment belonging to these guys. Am I right?"

I just nodded. This was getting interesting.

"Well, what if it were the scoring machines, not the wires or swords, that were broken or somehow damaged?" he continued.

"Could a problem with the scoring machines produce results like these?" I asked quickly, pointing to the list in Alan's hand.

"Definitely," he replied. "It would look as if everyone's equipment was broken."

"How could the officials discover the problem?" I asked.

Easy," Alan answered with a shrug. "All they have to do is check the equipment on another scoring machine."

Of course! How could I have been so thick? It had never occurred to me to ask Joe to check his equipment on another scoring machine.

"Who owns the machines?" I wanted to know.

"The host school," Alan replied. "In this case it would be Fieldview, obviously."

Well, I didn't have to think about who we would be checking in with next. We immediately took off to look for Fieldview's coach, Hank Jameson.

"Do you think it's a coincidence that Joe Repa was one of the disqualified fencers?" Nina asked me.

"No way!" Ollie cut in. "I think the culprit did Joe in so that Alan could win. He realized that it would be too easy to nail him if his tactics were discovered, so he sabotaged six other fencers to cover himself."

"Ol, I know Joe's your friend, but I wouldn't jump to that conclusion," I said. "We have a lot more work to do before we can possibly understand the real motive. Alan has given us an important clue. Now we need to establish whether it was each fencer's equipment that was malfunctioning or whether it was Fieldview's scoring machines."

"Really, Ollie, think about it," Nina piped up. "How would the culprit get access to equipment belonging to twenty-seven different fencers without any of them knowing anything about it?"

"In the locker room," Ollie replied with a shrug. He didn't sound so sure, though. "It's hard not to think Alan Flynn isn't behind this," Ollie continued. "After all, none of the other suspects are top fencers."

As Ollie was talking, I was suddenly struck by a whole new idea. Why were we assuming that the culprit was a fencer? Time was running out—we had to pick up the pace of this investigation fast.

"Ollie, take this list and find as many as you can of the twenty-seven other fencers who were affected," I ordered. "Ask them which strips they were fencing on. Maybe we can make a connection."

"Ten-four, Jackie," Ollie replied as he took off with the list.

Nina and I went to find Joe and test his equipment. Just as I had suspected, Joe's equipment was fine. The machines were the problem, half of them (strips 1 through 4) turned out to be broken.

"Now we should go talk to Coach Jameson," I told Nina. "He may prove to be the key to understanding how those machines came to be broken."

"What can I do for you?" Coach Jameson asked after Nina and I had introduced ourselves.

"Well, sir," I began, "could you tell me how long Fieldview has had those scoring machines? They seem fairly old."

"That's because they are," the coach replied. "In fact, we bought those machines the year I started at Fieldview, fifteen years ago. So far, they have never given us any trouble, though."

"But sir," Nina piped up, "don't you think seven dis-qualifications and twenty warnings are a little unusual?"

The coach nodded. "Don't get me wrong, kids, I realize it's a very bizarre occurrence. I've been fencing for about forty-three years and I've never seen anything like this. But there's one thing you have to understand. I personally check those machines before every bout. We don't want Fieldview getting a reputation for having shoddy scoring equipment. We wouldn't be asked to host any more meets and we'd certainly be losers in the eyes of our division of the U.S. Fencing Association. I repeat, I know for a fact that the equipment was in perfect working order early this morning."

"How early, Coach?" I asked.

"On the day of a big meet, like the one today, I'm here as early as six o'clock in the morning," he replied. "By seven, I had checked everything out already."

For a moment, I was stumped. But I'm never at a loss for words for long. "Do you also set up the strips and scoring tables?" I continued.

"No, I let my assistant, George Hoffman, handle that job," the coach replied. "He works for me part time."

Something in the coach's voice bothered me. "Has he been your assistant for long?" I asked.

Before the coach answered he surprised me by rolling his eyes. "Too long," he finally replied. Now, *that* was a revealing response.

"Where can I find Mr. Hoffman?" I asked Coach Jameson.

He directed us to the other side of the gym, where we found George Hoffman storing gear in the equipment closet. He jumped when I said his name. Obviously, he hadn't heard us approach.

"Nice to meet you, kids," Mr. Hoffman said. Much younger than Coach Jameson, he was outgoing and very friendly. "Having any luck with your case?" he asked. With a wink, he added, "Most of us would like to get home some time today, after all."

I ignored the slight dig at how long it was taking to solve this case and got to the point. I'm used to this kind of flak from adults, so I try not to take it personally. "I understand, Mr. Hoffman," I began, in my most formal detective tone, "that Coach Jameson has you put out the machinery for meets, is that right?"

Mr. Hoffman seemed a little irritated by the way I had phrased my question. "Sounds to me like you already know the answer to that, kid," he replied gruffly. "That's one of my jobs—to set up the equipment, such as it is."

"What do you mean 'such as it is?'" I had to ask.

"Well, you know, it's antiquated," he replied quickly, as if what he was saying was the most obvious thing in the world. "There's some great state-of-the-art stuff available, and, well . . ." Hoffman paused as if making sure to choose exactly the right words. "But it works," he finally continued. "In fact, Jameson teaches the kids how to maintain all of the equipment. Every member of the Fieldview fencing team knows how to work those scoring machines."

Nina and I looked at each other. This case was getting more and more complicated by the second.

Nina voiced the same thought that was crossing my mind. "Sir, do you think it's possible that a member of the Fieldview team deliberately tampered with several of the scoring machines today?" she asked. "Before the meet, I mean, and after Coach Jameson had completed his check?"

Hoffman wrinkled his forehead, listening closely to the question. "Well," he replied slowly, as if deep in thought, "most members of the team would certainly know how to cause a machine to malfunction, but I don't know who would want to do that."

"Do *you* know how to maintain the machines, Mr.

Hoffman?" I asked, watching his face closely.

"Sure," he said with a smile, "I'm the assistant coach." Yeah, right, I thought. I didn't like his smile one single bit. It was a mouth-only kind of smile. His eyes, which were blue and beady, didn't look at all sincere.

Nina and I thanked Hoffman for his time, but as we started to walk away, I turned to ask him one more question. "Sir, I understand that coaching is a part time job for you. What do you do the rest of the time?"

Hoffman cleared his throat. "I'm a salesman," he said.

"Thanks, Coach," I concluded. When I reached out to shake his hand, I noticed a bandage at the base of his left thumb. It looked like a nasty wound because blood was seeping through the bandage. "That looks painful," I commented.

"It's nothing," Mr. Hoffman replied quickly. "I just cut myself this morning on a broken blade."

"Well, I hope it heals quickly," I said. "See you around."

Nina and I went back across the gym to find Ollie. Then the three of us sat in a huddle on the bleachers to discuss what we knew. Next to each bout on the list, Ollie had marked the number of the strip on which the bout had taken place. Evidently, the victims had fenced on strips 1 through 4. It seemed apparent that the problem was with the machines and not with the individual fencers' equipment.

"Jack," Nina said, glancing up at me after checking her watch, "we only have about forty minutes left."

I didn't need Nina to tell me that time was running out.

We had less than an hour and still no key suspect. This was one tough case. Plus, I kept seeing images of Joe Repa's sad face. We had to crack this one. We just had to.

"From what Hoffman told you, it sounds as if anyone on the Fieldview team could have messed with those machines," Ollie said, scuffing his high-top against the bleachers. "If Coach Jameson teaches his fencers how to maintain the equipment, what do you want to bet that every other coach in the county does the same thing?"

"Don't be so sure, Ol," I retorted. "Jameson seems like an unusual kind of guy to me. Listen, could you find Joe Repa and bring him up here? I need to ask him a few more questions . . . without an audience."

Nina and Ollie looked at me and then at each other. They both raised their eyebrows. "Hey, guys," I continued, "just wait and see. I think we may all be in for a few surprises." I love being mysterious—it's all part of the game.

"Whatever you say, J.D.," Ollie finally said with a smile. Ollie loves to kid around with me. J.D., which stands for Jack Detective, is one of many nicknames he has given me. "Joe's probably in the locker room. I'll be right back." With that, he sped down the bleachers.

Nina and I sat in silence for a few minutes.

"I know that expression, Jack," Nina finally said. "What are you thinking?"

I had to smile. Nina is one good detective. "Let's just say," I replied, "that I am ninety-nine percent sure that the culprit is someone associated with Fieldview—a fencer, a janitor, someone who has access to the team's equipment."

"Go on," Nina prodded, her black eyes studying me seriously.

"I also feel confident that the crime occurred sometime very early this morning," I continued, "but after the machines were tested."

"Hey, guys, I'm back," Ollie announced loudly, climbing the bleacher steps two at a time. "What are you doing—solving this case without the incredible Steele mind? Impossible." Ollie proceeded to plop down rather gracelessly next to us.

"Where is Joe, Ollie?" I asked.

Ollie just smiled.

"Ol, this isn't funny," I prodded. "Time is of the essence, my man. Where is Joe?"

"Get a grip, Jack," Ollie replied. "Actually, you'll be interested to know that Joe and some of his teammates are eavesdropping on a heated discussion as we speak. He'll be up in a second."

"Whose discussion?" I wanted to know. "And why the heat?"

"Between Jameson and Hoffman," Ollie replied. "We can ask Joe about the heat when he gets here."

"Fine. Now, before we can point a finger at anyone, we need to prove that those four machines were faulty," I said. "Nina, could you let Mr. Magnuson know that we would like to examine the scoring machines?" I continued. "We should have his approval before we inspect them."

"Yes, sir," said Nina with a small bow. She likes to pretend that I'm too bossy, but secretly I think she doesn't really mind it at all. She knows that when I start giving orders it means that I'm on the way to solving a case.

Most of the spectators had gone. The only people left in the gym were the fencers, coaches, scouts and bout committee officials. They were all waiting for the results of our investigation. Talk about pressure! But pressure is what it's all about when you're a high level investigator like me.

"Well, Ollie," I began, turning to my associate. "I've ruled out the possibility that someone actually went to the trouble of damaging twenty-seven fencers' equipment, including Joe's."

Right on cue, Joe began to climb up the bleachers toward us. "Hi, Jack," Joe said. "Ollie mentioned that you wanted to talk to me about something."

"That's right, Joe," I replied. "I'm summing up all of the evidence we have. We have a number of suspects and I'm afraid the list just keeps growing."

Joe's face fell. "Oh," he said. "I was hoping you would tell me that you had solved the mystery."

"Don't worry, Joe," I reassured him. "Something tells me we're very close. But I need your help."

"Just name it," Joe said. "I'll do anything if it means I'll have a chance of a rematch."

I proceeded to tell Joe about our theory that the scoring machines were tampered with, not the fencers' equipment. "We also know that all of you Fieldview fencers are capable of repairing those machines," I added.

"Or, able to make them break down," Joe commented.

"Exactly," I replied. "Now, as I understand it, all of the

machines in use today belong to Fieldview."

"That's right," Joe responded. "We have eight of them. To my knowledge, they all worked just fine until today."

"My theory is that someone got his or her hands on four of those machines sometime after Coach Jameson tested them and before the start of today's competition," I explained. "To me, that narrows it down to the members of the Fieldview team. And I guess I can't rule out the coaches."

"Hey, guys," Nina suddenly interrupted, waving and calling to us from the gym floor. "Mr. Magnuson says it's O.K."

Ollie, Joe and I joined Nina by one of the machines that had malfunctioned.

"We'd better hurry," Nina warned, biting her lip anxiously. "There isn't much time left."

"I know, Nina," I replied. Nina is also sometimes quite the master at stating the obvious. "Joe, this is where you come in," I continued, turning to face Joe. "Since you are familiar with the equipment, maybe you can tell how the connections were broken."

With Joe's help, we examined all four of the machines that had malfunctioned.

"Whoa, Joe," Ollie commented after a few minutes of close scrutiny of the machines, "these machines are pretty old, aren't they? They look like fossils."

"Well, they certainly are less than state-of-the-art," Joe agreed, "but they've worked fine for us until now."

Why did that phrase, "state-of-the-art," echo in my mind?

"I will say this though," Joe continued, "these machines are not nearly as cool as the ones Hoffman is trying to turn Coach Jameson onto."

I stopped in my tracks, my heart pounding. "'Turn him onto?'" I repeated.

"Yeah," Joe replied. "Hoffman only works for us part time. His other job is selling fencing equipment for some sporting goods company. He keeps trying to get Coach to pick up some new equipment."

"Like scoring machines?" I asked. I had a feeling that I already knew the answer.

"Uh-huh," Joe replied. "But Coach doesn't think we need new equipment."

"Joe, what were the coaches arguing about a little while ago?" I asked.

"The same thing they always argue about," Joe said, fingering one of the metal boxes, "these old contraptions. Hoffman thinks that if Coach had gotten some of his state-of-the-art models, we would never have run into the problems we had today. . . . Hey, guys, look at this. There's blood on this machine."

Joe pointed to the edge of the box where the metal on the top surface had split apart from the metal side of the box. The edge was like the blade of a sharp knife—and the blood was plain to see. Someone had apparently been very careless.

"What time is it, Nina?" I asked.

"Six-fifty," Nina replied solemnly.

"Well, this is it," I said in my most confident tone of

voice, looking from one of my associates to the other.

"What is it?" Nina and Ollie asked at the same time.

"You'll see," I said mysteriously. "Joe, could you go get your coaches and ask them to join us at the Bout Committee table? Tell them that Mr. Magnuson would like to talk to them."

"Sure, Jack," Joe replied, looking confused.

"Ollie, unhook that machine, please," I said, pointing to the one Joe had just been examining. "Let's go talk to Mr. Magnuson. I think he's going to be very happy with what we have to tell him."

"What do we have to tell him, Jack?" Ollie asked. I brushed his question aside—I was concentrating all of my energy on my confrontation speech.

Δ   Δ   Δ

"Ah, we were just about to do our final tally of the bout results," Mr. Magnuson informed me as our little group descended on him. "It is seven o'clock, you know."

"Right on time," I replied. "We've solved the case, Mr. Magnuson."

Ollie and Nina looked at me. They hate it when I don't clue them in beforehand, but sometimes a detective's got to do what he's got to do. Time constraints and all that. Just then, Joe and the two Fieldview coaches joined us.

"Well, it became clear to us fairly quickly—with Alan Flynn's help—that it wasn't Joe's equipment, or the equipment of the other disqualified fencers, that was faulty," I began my summary. "It was the scoring machines—the ones on strips one through four, to be exact.

"Now, I know Coach Jameson is very careful about keeping those scoring machines in good working condition. He checked them himself at six this morning." I turned to face the coach. He nodded. "I don't doubt that he was telling the truth.

"However, Coach Jameson did not actually set up the gym for today's competition, did you, sir?" I continued.

"No, I did not," the coach answered.

"I did. So what?" Mr. Hoffman exclaimed.

"Just a second," I said, turning to face Hoffman. "I also learned this afternoon that your part-time coaching job leaves you plenty of time for another career, doesn't it, Mr. Hoffman?" I asked.

"Hey, a guy's got to make a living," Mr. Hoffman responded with a sneer. "There's no crime in that." Gone was the very friendly guy we had met earlier.

"Mr. Hoffman sells fencing equipment," I informed Mr. Magnuson, who looked a bit baffled. "I imagine scoring machines are his most expensive item. If you sold, say, eight of them, or better yet, if you sold state-of-the-art scoring machines to schools across the county, well, you'd probably make a pretty nice commission. Is that a fair guess, Mr. Hoffman?"

"Just what is it that you're getting at, kid?" Hoffman demanded.

I chose to ignore his question. Sometimes that's the only thing to do when suspects are getting angry. Anyway, I thought I was making myself pretty clear. "Notice that Mr. Hoffman has a nasty cut on his hand that he claims was caused by a broken blade. I don't think so. I believe that he got that cut while tampering with one of four scoring machines. If he had gotten away with it, the publicity from today's series of warnings and disqualifications would have been great for his business. Chances are, several fencing programs would have updated their equipment for fear of tarnishing fencing's sterling reputation for chivalry and valor. George Hoffman was planning to profit quite nicely from that fear," I concluded.

"It would have worked if it weren't for you meddling kids," Hoffman blurted out. He glared at us. I have to admit that I was kind of glad that I was surrounded by a group of people. Hoffman looked pretty mad.

"That sounds like a confession to me," Mr. Magnuson said. "We'll start with seven rematches first thing tomorrow."

Joe started to grin as he clapped me on the back. We all watched as Coach Jameson started to give Mr. Hoffman a large piece of his mind.

"Looks like Coach Jameson will be needing a new assistant," Nina said, as we walked away.

"Are you kidding?" Joe commented with a laugh. "He won't let anyone within a mile of his precious equipment from now on."

Δ   Δ   Δ

The next morning, Ollie and I were shooting hoops in my office—I mean, my driveway—before we left for the fencing rematches.

"That was a great job we did yesterday," Ollie said as

he dribbled the ball around me for a clear shot.

"Yeah," I agreed as I tried to get the ball away from him. "I think two hours may be our best time for solving a case."

"Do you think Hoffman will stay in the sporting goods business?" Ollie asked.

"Well, after yesterday's incident, I don't know who would want a guy like that selling their goods," I replied, getting the ball away from Ollie and shooting wildly for the basket. The ball didn't even come near the rim. Ah, well, Michael Jordan I'm not.

"I wonder what makes a person do such awful stuff," Ollie continued. "He could have cost Joe a college scholarship. What a sleaze!"

"I guess greed can make you do some pretty terrible things," I told him. "We can only hope that if we hadn't caught up with him, his conscience would have."

"We can only hope," Ollie repeated, sinking the ball through the hoop for two points.

Case closed!

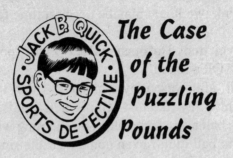

The Case
of the
Puzzling
Pounds

It wasn't really much of a wrestling match—yet. The Fieldview Bobcats had a 15-9 lead over Hamilton Military Academy. But that could change at any moment. And now Randy Quinn was taking his place on the wrestling mat for HMA. Randy Quinn was last year's county champion in the 132-pound weight class, and was already this year's favorite. Randy has a reputation for pinning just about everyone he wrestles, and a pin in this match would give HMA six points to tie the score, and the Academy some much needed momentum. A pin occurs when both of a wrestler's shoulders are touching the mat for a count of three seconds.

Both teams had perfect 9-0 records coming into this meet, but HMA was lagging now. Randy's opponent was the Bobcats' Joe Hillman, who was just stepping onto the mat himself. He was swinging his arms and torso back and forth, trying to loosen up his muscles for this match.

"Hey, Nina," I said, nudging her with my right elbow. Nina Chin is one of my associates on the Jack B. Quick Detective Squad. Ollie Steele, sitting on my left, is my other associate. Oh, and by the way, I'm Jack. "Didn't Kenny say that Dave Burton was cutting down a weight class to go against Randy Quinn?" I asked Nina. Kenny Chin is one of Nina's cousins, and he wrestles in the 119-pound class for the Bobcats. He and Dave Burton are best friends. Dave is the two-time county champ in the 138-pound class.

"That's what he told me," Nina replied. "He said that Coach Green asked Dave to go down to 132 because he had wrestled that weight class during summer camp and had beaten Randy Quinn. In fact, Dave pinned him. Randy wasn't too pleased about that."

Her eyebrows furrowed over her dark, almost black eyes as she looked over at Dave on the Fieldview bench. He was sitting next to Kenny with a towel wrapped around his neck, underneath the hood of his warm-up jacket.

"He's suited up to wrestle," Nina pointed out. "And I know he worked hard to lose those six pounds because Kenny helped him. Dave has grown so much recently that it was hard for him to just stay at 138, much less get below it."

"You know, six pounds doesn't sound like too much to lose," Ollie commented. "But it must seem like a ton when you *have* to lose it in a set amount of time."

"Kenny says it's tough enough just to maintain your weight," Nina responded. "But he was pretty sure Dave would make it."

Our conversation ended as the fans from HMA stood up with a loud roar. Randy had moved in swiftly on Joe Hillman and lifted him up slightly off the mat, which enabled Randy to take Joe down and score two points.

"Joe seems to be having a little trouble," I said, stating the obvious.

Joe was fighting hard, but Randy was working harder to flip him. The strain was evident on both of their faces. And this was only the first of three two-minute periods.

Suddenly, the Fieldview fans were shouting. Joe had spun quickly around and was able to escape from Randy's hold. Joe was awarded a point for his escape, bringing the score to 2-1. If Joe had been able to gain control over his opponent as well as escape his hold, he would have scored another point and tied Randy. This is called a reversal.

At the start of the second period, Joe got on his hands and knees and Quinn positioned himself above and behind him in the referee's position. The second and third periods of the match are begun in this way—the first is started with the wrestlers standing. Quinn's right arm was wrapped around Joe's stomach while his left hand was holding Joe's left elbow.

When the whistle blew, Joe scored another point by escaping one more time from Randy's clutching hold, tying the score. Fans were wildly waving blue and white banners—Fieldview's colors. From that point on, Randy and Joe were in a deadlock and the referee had to separate them frequently. Each move one made was skillfully countered by the other.

"This is intense!" Nina gasped, forgetting about Dave for the moment. She was so into the match that I doubt she realized that she was clutching my arm so tightly that it was just about cutting off the circulation.

"It sure is," Ollie agreed. "I didn't think Joe stood a chance, but he's fighting hard in there."

"He's wrestling the match of his life," I said, also impressed. "I hope he can keep this up for the last period as well."

Since Ollie and I have started coming to Kenny's meets with Nina, I've learned that wrestling is a grueling sport of endurance and skill. In the three periods, each wrestler attempts to pin his opponent's shoulders to the mat. He also tries to score points in the event that he *doesn't* pin his opponent. If neither wrestler is pinned, then the wrestler with the greater number of points at the end of the match wins.

However, if the score is tied at the end of the match, each wrestler is awarded two points, which are added to their teams' total scores.

I've also learned that there are several different weight classes in which a wrestler can compete. They range from 98 pounds to more than 185, which is considered heavyweight. Each wrestler must "make weight," which means that he must be weighed in at, or under, the level that he chooses to wrestle. This is to ensure fairness and safety in all matches.

The match between Joe Hillman and Randy Quinn was the closest I had ever seen. Both wrestlers were gritting their teeth in frustration because neither could overcome the other. Finally, Randy took the lead by escaping from the low spot of the referee's position. From there, both Randy and Joe remained locked in various holds until the timekeeper threw the sock on the mat. This indicated the end of the match, and the winner was Randy, by a score of 3-2.

The Fieldview crowd cheered for Joe despite his loss. He had avoided being pinned by Randy and had been able to maintain a crucial four-point lead for Fieldview.

Dave Burton gave Joe a high-five as he shed his warm-ups to wrestle HMA's Jimmy Marcus. Jimmy had been Dave's rival for the past four years.

"You know, maybe Coach Green had a change in strategy," Ollie said thoughtfully. "Like, he wanted to psyche Randy Quinn out or something. You know, by making him think he was going to wrestle Dave Burton."

"Then why did Dave work so hard to lose all that weight?" I asked, playing the devil's advocate to Ollie's suggestion.

"Perhaps," Nina jumped in, countering my question, "Coach Green saw how hard it was for Dave to lose the weight and decided to leave things as they were."

Our speculation ended there as the referee's whistle blew, signaling the start of the bout. Dave jumped in and took Jimmy down, but Jimmy was quick and immediately had a reversal. However, Dave was ready for this and was able to escape within seconds.

The crowd was roaring like crazy at the action. At the end of the first period, both wrestlers were sucking air.

Dave had a one-point lead and had selected the top spot

of the referee's position. He is excellent at riding an opponent and tiring him out from this position.

"Watch this," Nina said, nudging my arm and knocking me right into Ollie. "Dave should take control now." Nina gets really excited at these events, and often she doesn't realize her own strength. Her enthusiastic nudge had almost started the domino effect down our bench on the bleachers.

A murmur rose from the crowd as, to everyone's surprise, Jimmy did a quick roll and reversed Dave almost immediately. Dave seemed just as surprised as the crowd. Everyone could see that he had a dazed and confused look on his face as he lay beneath Jimmy.

Dave was able to escape just before the end of the period, but he couldn't make anything else work. His reversal attempts were stifled by Jimmy almost as soon as Dave blinked. And in the last seconds, as he tried to take Jimmy down, he wasn't able to budge him an inch.

"Dave isn't looking so hot, huh?" I observed. "He's got no zip!"

"The dude just doesn't have it!" Ollie cut in, shaking his head.

"Well, I hope he can get his head together for the last period," Nina said hopefully.

"At least Dave managed to tie the score," I added.

As the third period started, Dave seemed to have gained back some strength. He escaped from Jimmy's hold almost immediately, gaining a 1 point lead, 5-4. Then, in the final seconds, Jimmy grabbed at Dave's ankle and kicked out the other one while pouncing on top of Dave.

"Oh, no!" Nina cried. "Not a takedown! Now Jimmy's in the lead."

Dave tried hard, straining every muscle in his body, but he wasn't able to escape. Jimmy still had a tight hold on him from behind as the sock hit the mat. When Dave stood up, there was blood running down his face. I watched him walk over to the bench. One of his teammates tossed him a towel and he held it to his nose. The Fieldview coach came over, looked at Dave's nose, and plugged it with a cotton ball. Then Dave walked back to the mat.

The referee took hold of both of the wrestlers' arms, but raised Jimmy's. The HMA fans went wild. Their team had started to catch up with Fieldview. The score was now tied at 15 each.

"Something must have happened to Dave," said a disappointed Nina. "After Jimmy reversed him in the second period, he looked as if he had lost it. But there's no way he could lose to Jimmy. He hasn't lost to him—ever." She emphasized this last point by pounding her fist on my knee.

"Well, he didn't have his usual winning form, that's for sure," Ollie said, rubbing his hair, which is cut in a high-top fade.

"Hey," I said to Nina. "Things happen. As an athlete, you should know that you can't win them all."

"But you saw his nose bleeding, Jack," Nina said. "The same thing happened to Kenny when he dropped to the 119 weight class. He crash-dieted so much that he had a nose bleed. And when he finally stepped on the scale, he realized he was a few pounds *under*weight."

"Underweight?" I echoed, readjusting my glasses.

"Yes," she replied. "I think that Dave may have been wrestling at the wrong weight."

Looking at the bench, I saw that Dave still had a dazed expression on his face. He didn't seem to have accepted what had happened.

Nina was still upset, and I couldn't help thinking that she was getting a little ahead of herself by thinking that something had happened to Dave. Still, there was something nagging at the back of my mind that told me she might be onto a case.

When the final match was over, HMA was on top, 22-21. Dave's loss to Jimmy had been the turning point because it had given HMA the momentum it needed to take the lead. Fieldview's unexpected loss made me start thinking more seriously about Nina's suspicions.

We made our way down to see Kenny Chin and congratulate him on his victory. On the way, we bumped into Coach Green. He was barrel-shaped with a powerful-looking chest and huge forearms. I could tell just by looking at him that he must have been a feared wrestler in his day.

"Hi, Coach," I greeted him. "I'm Jack B. Quick, sports detective. These are my associates, Nina Chin and Ollie Steele."

Coach Green smiled and turned to Nina. "Are you related to Kenny Chin?"

"He's my cousin," Nina replied. She seemed happy to be recognized as a relation. Even more so, I imagined, since Kenny had won his match.

"You should be proud," Coach Green told her. "Kenny's a great wrestler. I expect he'll make the top five at the county championships."

"That would be great!" Nina exclaimed. "I'm curious," she went on in her blunt way. "Is it true that you were planning on having Dave Burton face Randy Quinn in the 132 class?"

Obviously, Nina was completely serious about investigating this business about Dave.

"Yes, that was the plan, but Dave didn't make weight," the coach replied after a pause. "Had I known that Joe was going to wrestle the way he did, I wouldn't have asked Dave to go down. Cutting weight can really sap your energy."

"Could there have been an error during the weigh-in?" Nina asked, continuing her investigation.

"That's not possible," replied the coach firmly. "We just got a brand new scale yesterday." Coach Green explained that the team's old scale had broken about two weeks earlier, and that they had been without a scale while the new one was on order.

"The boys have been weighing themselves at home," he went on. "Dave seemed confident that he would make weight, but when he weighed in, he was two pounds over." Coach Green shrugged. "I had no choice but to wrestle him at 138."

"Could the fact that Dave had lost some weight have affected his ability to wrestle at his usual weight?" I asked.

"It certainly could have," Coach Green said, frowning. "It could have affected his strength, endurance and even up here," he finished, tapping his temple with his finger. "If your mental preparation is off," he explained to us, "it can really throw you in a match."

I remembered the dazed look that had been on Dave's face while he wrestled Jimmy. He had been preparing himself to wrestle Randy Quinn, and at the last minute, with the switch to Jimmy Marcus, Dave must have lost some of his edge.

I noticed Nina staring at me sidelong, and Ollie too. We had been working together long enough to realize what the others were thinking. Perhaps someone hadn't wanted Dave to wrestle at 132. And perhaps this same person knew that if he tried to lose the weight, he wouldn't be up to par in 138 either.

"Coach," I spoke up after a brief moment of silence. "We think it's possible that someone didn't want Dave Burton to wrestle at 132. Would you mind if we looked into it?"

"If Dave doesn't mind, I have no objections," the coach replied. "I have to admit, I'm a bit curious myself."

The team had already gone into the locker room, so Nina, Ollie and I waited for Dave to emerge. When he finally did, we pulled him aside and told him about our conversation with Coach Green.

"To tell you the truth, guys," he said, sitting down on the bleachers, "I'm really upset about losing to Jimmy Marcus. That dude never should have beaten me."

"Doesn't it bother you that you missed weigh-in by two pounds?" Ollie asked. "You must be disappointed—especially since you starved yourself for two weeks."

"Yeah, I guess it does bother me," he said with a shrug. "I worked so hard to lose that weight. I ran in a rubber suit, jumped rope and everything," Dave continued, raising his eyebrows for emphasis. "Heck, I even sucked on ice cubes instead of eating lunch."

He shook his head and then looked up at us. We were standing around him in a semicircle. Kenny Chin was there too, waiting to drive Nina and the rest of us home.

"You guys really think there's something more to this?" he finally asked us, skeptically.

Kenny spoke up. "My cousin here," he said, patting Nina on the head, "has been doing this detective stuff for a long time with her friends. I believe them."

"Well, then," Dave said and nodded. "Go ahead with your investigation."

"For starters, Dave," I began, "when you weighed yourself at home, did your weight tend to vary much?"

"Actually," Dave replied, "I didn't weigh myself at home. The scale at my house is older than I am, and my parents play with it to make themselves feel better about not dieting. So I've been using the scale in the nurse's office at school. As far as I could tell, my weight was pretty consistent."

"There was one point when we thought Dave had hit a wall, though," Kenny added. "During the last few days, it seemed like he'd never break 133. We figured a little extra running would do it."

"Yeah, I was one pound over for the longest time,"

Dave said, recalling his weight struggle. "Then, two days before the weigh-in, I finally got down to 132. I figured I could stay at 132 once I reached it, but I ended up gaining two pounds instead."

"Were you the only one on the team using the nurse's scale?" I asked Dave, pushing my glasses up on my nose.

"As far as I know, yeah," Dave replied.

"And who, besides Kenny, knew that you were using it?"

"Just the nurse and Gina," he responded, brushing his wet brown hair into place with his hand. He explained that Gina is his ex-girlfriend. "I broke up with Gina four days ago. She was dieting too, but I was losing weight a lot faster than she was. Gina was pretty jealous about it, and when I hit the wall, she kept telling me I'd never make it. That was the last thing I needed to hear."

"What about Joe Hillman?" Nina asked, tucking a stray strand of hair into her long braid. "Was he upset when Coach Green asked you to go down to 132? I mean, if you had made weight in his weight class, he wouldn't have wrestled today."

"I guess so. But Joe was pretty cool about it," Dave replied. "He grumbled about it for a while, but I guess he realized the coach wasn't going to change his mind."

"Coach Green said that the team's scale was broken," Ollie added, pushing up the sleeves of his black and royal blue track jacket. "Is there any chance that someone might have broken it deliberately?"

"I hadn't even thought about it," Kenny replied,

surprised. "But with a rivalry like the one we have with HMA, it wouldn't surprise me if someone from over there had something to do with it."

"You know, now that I think about it, Jimmy Marcus muttered something to me at the end of the second period," Dave said, tilting his head as if in deep thought. "It was something really nasty like,'I'm gonna break your knees, Burton!' It really surprised me."

"Speaking of the match, Dave," Nina said. "You seemed pretty worn out from the second period on. What happened?"

"I kind of hit bottom after Jimmy reversed me. My arms felt dead and my legs were like rubber bands," Dave explained. "It took me a while to get back into it, and that's when I finally escaped. I never really felt one hundred percent after that."

We thanked Dave for his time, and then Kenny drove us all back to my house. We needed to discuss what was turning out to be *The Case of the Puzzling Pounds*.

We decided to split up the next day to continue our investigation. Nina would talk to Gina Taylor, Dave's ex-girlfriend, to see what she could learn. Perhaps Gina had messed with the scale in a fit of jealousy.

Ollie would talk to Joe Hillman, even though Dave thought that Joe had eventually accepted Coach Green's strategy. I believe in covering all the angles—even the unlikely ones.

The next day it was raining, so I took the bus over to HMA and waited for a chance to talk to Jimmy Marcus. I caught Jimmy as he was walking out of the locker room after practice.

At 5'7", Jimmy is tall for his weight class. His long legs give him leverage over his opponents, and had definitely helped him overcome Dave Burton. His brown hair was plastered to his head, since he had just come from the shower. Somehow, seeing him with his hair like that made him a lot less intimidating. However, his gray military school uniform was anything but reassuring.

"Hey, Jimmy," I called out. "Have you got a minute?"

He turned to see who was calling him, said good-bye to his friends and came over to where I was standing. "Do I know you?" he asked, looking me over.

"I'm Jack B. Quick," I said, smiling and shaking his hand. "I saw you in yesterday's match against Fieldview and you were great!" I hoped my enthusiasm would get him to warm up to me.

"Thanks," he replied. "So what can I do for you?"

"I know that you had never beaten Dave Burton before yesterday," I began, not yet mentioning that I was a detective, "and I was wondering if you had done anything differently to beat him."

"Well, Jack," Jimmy replied, after tugging on his lower lip for a moment, "the most important thing for me was to forget about all the times Burton had beaten me. Mental prep is key. You see, if you're convinced the other guy will win just because he's won before, then there's really no sense in wrestling the match at all."

"You mean you knew that you would win from the start

of the match?" I asked, adjusting my glasses.

"No, but I had to *think* I would," he corrected me. "And lucky for me, Burton didn't seem to be in such good shape yesterday. Otherwise, he probably would have beaten me."

As we talked, I grew to like Jimmy Marcus. He appeared to have genuine respect for Dave Burton's ability as a wrestler. I dreaded doing it, but I still had to ask him my next question. It was a necessary part of the investigation.

"Is that why you told Dave that you were going to break his knees?" I asked, trying to maintain eye contact.

"Who told you that? Dave?" Jimmy asked, his eyes narrowing suspiciously. "What's going on here?"

I explained to him about the weigh-in and the broken scale and how we had begun the investigation.

"I beat Dave Burton fair and square," Jimmy exclaimed angrily, his green eyes blazing. "Do you think that *I* had something to do with the broken scale? What would that have done for me? Word was that Burton was cutting weight to go up against Randy Quinn. If he had lost that weight, I would have gained a definite victory against Chuck Oaks."

I knew that Oaks was Dave's back-up at 138 pounds and I guessed that Jimmy was probably right about that victory. "What about Randy Quinn?" I asked, changing tactics. "Isn't it true that Dave beat Randy at the summer camp tournament?"

"Yeah, that's true," Jimmy replied, calming down. "Look, I said that to Dave to psyche him out. It wasn't personal. When you get pumped up like I was, you say things like that to intimidate your opponent." Jimmy stood up, grabbed his duffel bag and slung it over his shoulder.

"I gotta get going," he said. Without another word, he turned and left. As I watched Jimmy exit the gym, I decided to wait and talk to Randy Quinn as well. I sat down on the bleachers and watched the wrestlers walk out. I hadn't seen Randy leave yet, so I figured he must still be changing.

Randy was the last wrestler to leave the locker room. Even though he weighed only 132 pounds, he was built like a pitbull. It had just occurred to me that, although Jimmy had nothing to lose if Dave Burton wrestled at 132, Randy Quinn definitely *did*.

"Excuse me," I called, getting up from my seat on the bleachers, "aren't you Randy Quinn?"

Randy stopped to look me over, just as Jimmy had done, but Randy was a little more intimidating. "Yeah," was all he said. He stood there, flexing his muscles, waiting for me to say something else.

"I'm Jack B. Quick," I said, introducing myself.

Randy looked at me a little blankly, but then he blinked. "You're that kid detective, aren't you?" he asked. "What do you want with me?"

"Well, I saw you wrestle yesterday," I continued and then paused for a second.

"Well, what of it?" Randy asked, taking a step toward me. He is definitely not somebody I would ever want to meet in a dark alley, that's for sure.

"Do you think that Dave Burton would have beaten you if he had made weight?" I blurted out. There were times I really missed Nina and her blunt method of questioning.

Randy didn't look like the kind of guy who liked to beat around the bush.

"The only way to know is if he had made weight," Randy said, shrugging his shoulders. "But he didn't." With that, Randy turned to go.

I decided to get right to my next point. "Do you know anything about Fieldview's scale?" I asked Randy's retreating back.

Randy stopped and spun around. I breathed a sigh of relief. He didn't look angry—yet. If anything, he looked confused. "What about the scale?" he asked. Either he honestly didn't know, or he was a very good actor. I decided that the jury was still out on that one.

"Fieldview's scale broke two weeks ago," I went on, trying not to worry about whether I was going to have my head handed to me. "The school just got a new one two days ago."

"Well, there you have it, Jack," Randy replied. "That's probably why Burton didn't make the weight." He smiled for the first time. Have you ever seen a crocodile smile? Well, that's what Randy reminded me of.

I thanked Randy for his help and watched him walk out of the gym. I didn't think I'd get anything more out of him—not that I had actually gotten any new information from him in the first place.

During the bus ride home, I reflected on my conversations with Randy and Jimmy. I had a feeling that Randy might have heard about Fieldview's broken scale, but he had not wanted me to know and therefore include him as a suspect. My instinct was that he had not had anything to do with it, though. But, I couldn't rule out the possibility—yet.

While I waited for Ollie and Nina to show up at my house, I updated my computer file on *The Case of the Puzzling Pounds*. I had already typed in the interviews with Dave Burton, Coach Green and Kenny Chin, but for a case about weight, things were looking pretty slim. I hoped that Ollie and Nina would have something to beef things up.

They arrived within ten minutes of each other, eager to share the information they had obtained and see how everything might fit together. I filled them in on my interviews with Jimmy Marcus and Randy Quinn, and then Ollie told us about his talk with Joe Hillman.

"Joe's a nice guy, like Dave said," Ollie began. "I asked him how he felt when he heard that Dave was going down to 132. He admitted he was pretty angry."

"Was he angry enough to make sure that Dave didn't make weight?" Nina jumped in.

Ollie held his hand up like a traffic cop. "Yo, slow down, Nina. I'm getting to it—hold your horses," he teased.

"I was about to say," Ollie continued, running his hand over the top of his head, "that at first Joe was furious at Coach Green. He was never mad at Dave because he knew that Dave had about as much control over the decision as he did.

"Joe also said that no wrestler likes to lose weight when he doesn't have to. It's a lot of work with little reward, especially when dessert gets served," Ollie said with a laugh.

"Anyway," he went on, "Joe said he knew that being

angry wasn't going to change things. He decided it would be better if he showed Coach Green that he would do whatever was necessary to help the team win. And if it meant sitting out a match, Joe said he was prepared to do that."

"But then he didn't have to," I commented softly. We definitely could not rule Joe out as a suspect just because he had come off like a good sport in front of Ollie.

"Where did Joe weigh himself?" Nina asked, glancing at me. She loves beating me to questions. I hadn't even switched to that gear yet, and Nina knew it.

"Always at home," Ollie replied. I typed it in. "And I checked his class schedule—I got that from Coach Green. While I waited for their practice to end, I wandered the halls and located his classrooms. None of them is anywhere near the nurse's office. Even his locker is at the other end of the school."

"Did you find out anything else?" I asked hopefully. So far, we were narrowing the field of suspects without gaining any new clues as to who the culprit might be. Investigations like this are like doing math homework—I'm good at it, but that doesn't mean that I like it.

Ollie shook his head slowly. "Not a thing," he sighed.

"Well," I said, typing in the last of Ollie's information and shrugging my shoulders, "let's hear about Gina Taylor." I looked at Nina, who seemed to be collecting mental notes on her talk. "What did Gina have to say?" I was worried that she might echo Ollie's last comment. Making something out of nothing is the toughest part about being an investigator.

"I noticed right away that Gina seemed pretty bitter

about the breakup," Nina began, a serious look on her face.

"But why did she keep telling Dave that he would never make the weight?" Ollie interjected.

"She said that she was sick and tired of hearing him complain about it all the time. And to top that off, he was hardly spending any time with her," Nina added, shooting Ollie a glance. She hates it when he interrupts her.

"Did you ask how her diet was going?" Ollie wanted to know, grinning widely.

"I was trying to get information from her, Ollie," Nina shot back. "Not get booted through a window."

"Is it true, though," I cut in, "that Dave was having more luck than Gina at losing weight?"

"Yeah," Nina responded immediately. "That is, until he hit that wall. And that was just before they broke up."

"So Gina knew about Dave's weigh-ins," I added over the clicking of my keyboard.

"She said she used to go with Dave when he weighed himself at the nurse's office. She kept records of both of their weights in a notebook."

"Didn't Dave ever have someone double-check his weight on the scale?" Ollie asked, a little incredulously.

"Why should he?" Nina replied. "I would think he could trust himself. But then, when he stopped losing weight, Gina told me that Dave had both she and Kenny check the scale's read-out. Otherwise, Dave just read the scale himself."

"Did Gina use that scale, too?" I asked, glancing up at Nina as I loaded the information. It saves so much time to type and listen simultaneously. I was definitely going to have to see about getting a portable computer.

"No, she used her own scale at home," Nina explained. "She weighed herself every morning before she got dressed."

That *was* interesting, I thought. If someone had tampered with the nurse's scale, it would definitely explain why Gina had been losing weight while Dave had stopped. But there was still the question of who had tampered with the scale.

"Did Gina say anything else, Nina?" I asked, breaking the silence.

"Yes," Nina replied. "She said she went to see the nurse about her weight loss program just before Dave hit the wall. She wanted to know if there was anything else she could do to shed some more weight."

"I almost forgot about the nurse," I said. "What's her name?"

"Mrs. Flanagan," Nina answered. "She, of course, knew that Dave was using the scale in her office. And the minute Gina asked about her diet, Mrs. Flanagan got really upset. She started yelling at Gina for worrying about her weight when she should be worrying about her health. She kept saying that dieting can be dangerous—especially if it's taken too far."

"Wow!" Ollie exclaimed. "That was really giving it to her. What did Gina do?"

Nina shrugged. "What could she do? She listened until Mrs. Flanagan let her leave."

"Sounds like Mrs. Flanagan has an attitude problem," Ollie commented, and then paused. "But then again, so many of those fad diets are totally unhealthy."

"That's true," I agreed. It *is* ridiculous how so many people buy into the whole "lose 30 pounds in five hours" kind of thing. As far as I understand it, reducing your caloric intake and exercising are the keys to safe weight loss.

Δ   Δ   Δ

The following afternoon, I headed over to the Fieldview nurse's office. It was time to check out her scale. I was carrying a five-pound dumbbell in my knapsack. My back was killing me.

The nurse was rolling bandages when I walked in. I know, I know. I thought they only did that in Civil War movies. But, I guess I was wrong.

"May I help you?" Mrs. Flanagan asked, looking up.

How was I going to check on her scale without letting her see me, I wondered. Suddenly, I realized that I was about to start feeling light-headed at any moment.

"Umm," I began, thinking quickly. I definitely should have thought this out before I got there. This case was really getting to me. "I was watching the . . . uh . . . wrestling team practice," I began, sticking as close to the facts as possible, "when I started feeling really weak." I closed my eyes and tried to think weak. I swayed a little, hoping that I would start to look feeble. The power of the mind over the body is an incredible thing. "They told me to come down here." I didn't have to tell her who "they" were. Leaving things as vague as possible is a very good idea in this type of situation.

Mrs. Flanagan bought it. She rushed over to help me to a cot. "You poor boy," she said, touching my forehead. "You feel kind of flushed. I'm going to get you a cool washcloth and a little ice. Don't go away."

As soon as she walked out of the office, I jumped up—instant recovery. I quickly pulled the dumbbell from my knapsack and put it on the scale. A few moments of trying to balance the levers, and I had definite proof that the scale was fixed. It read three pounds—two pounds too light.

I heard Mrs. Flanagan's footsteps in the hall outside the office. I grabbed my weight and practically leaped back onto the cot. Now all I had to do was to figure out who in the world would have fixed the nurse's scale—and how to get out of the nurse's clutches.

Δ   Δ   Δ

Sitting down at my computer that night, I went over the afternoon's events. After escaping from Mrs. Flanagan, I had headed back to the wrestling room. And now I had a new suspect: someone I hadn't even thought of before.

As I entered the information on the computer, I mulled over the conversation I had overheard at the end of practice. I had followed Dave and Kenny into the locker room, thinking I'd talk to the coach again in case there was anything I had missed.

I scratched my head thoughtfully as I read my transcript of the conversation on the computer screen.

"You know, Kenny," Dave had said. "I'm almost glad I didn't have to wrestle Randy last week."

"What are you talking about?" Kenny had asked, incredulously. "You beat him over the summer."

"I know I did," Dave had replied, "but the guy is nuts. You know what Jimmy told me? He said that Randy has been working out for four hours a day. He runs at least eight miles every night after practice, and he's benching almost twice as much as he did last year."

"Wow!" Kenny had exclaimed. "And Joe almost beat him?"

"I know, I know," Dave had answered. "That's pretty wild, isn't it? I'm really teed off, though, that I lost to Jimmy. There was no reason for that!"

They had seen me behind them at that point, and asked me how things were going. I was a little baffled, to say the least. I definitely had not picked Dave as someone with a cowardly side. But hey, everyone's full of surprises. It just made things so much more complicated. I did not know quite what to do yet. I was going to have to sleep on this.

Δ   Δ   Δ

Coach Green was on the phone the next afternoon when I walked into his office. After overhearing Dave the day before, I had never made it to talk to the coach.

"Listen, Mrs. Flanagan," he said into the receiver, obviously trying not to lose his patience. He rolled his eyes at me while motioning me to take a seat. "I understand your concern, but I have a practice to run here."

He paused and held the phone away from his ear. I could hear the nurse's voice from my chair, but I could not make out her words.

"I know it won't take long—" Coach Green began, but

was then cut off. He started tapping on his desk with the pencil he was holding.

"Well, how many other teams are you testing?" he finally got in. "What?" he asked after a brief pause.

Then there was a longer pause. I was very glad I wasn't the pencil the coach was holding because at that second, it snapped like a match stick.

"I'm not very happy about this, Mrs. Flanagan," Coach Green practically spat out. "But if the principal is behind you, then I guess I don't have much choice, do I?" He slammed the phone down and looked at me.

I raised my eyebrows, inviting him to share the conversation with me.

"That nurse wants to test all my boys for iron deficiencies," he said angrily. "Can you believe it?"

I didn't answer. I was too busy thinking of Dave's nosebleed after his match last week. And of something Mrs. Flanagan had said to Gina. I got up and shut the door. Coach Green and I had something important to talk about. I had solved the case. Now all I had to do was prove it.

Δ　　　Δ　　　Δ

An hour later, Nina, Ollie, Coach Green, Dave, Joe and I headed down to the nurse's office. After I had talked to the coach, we had Dave and Joe weigh themselves in the locker room. I had decided that a confrontational approach to this case was the best tactic.

Joe was 134, and Dave weighed just one pound over competition weight at 139.

When we got to the office, Dave, Joe and the coach

went inside. My squad and I waited outside in the hall for Coach Green's signal.

We heard the nurse greet them, and the coach explain that there was a problem with the new scale. This time, Joe weighed in at 132 exactly, while Dave was at 137. As we heard them reading off their weights, Coach Green called us inside.

"Mrs. Flanagan," the coach said once we were all in the office. "I think you have some explaining to do." He then told her about the discrepancies in the boys' weights, adding that he'd been lying about a problem with the new scale.

Once Mrs. Flanagan realized that we had proof, she confessed right away. She said that she had fixed the scale so that Dave would think he had lost the weight, when he was actually two pounds shy of his goal.

"Why did you do this?" Dave asked in confusion. "I was working so hard to lose that weight. Why did you trick me like that?"

The nurse explained that she couldn't stand to see the way the wrestlers starve themselves to make weight. She feels that it is very unhealthy, especially when they are still growing boys. She told us that she had tried to talk to the coach about it, but he had never listened. But now, she had permission to get everyone tested for iron deficiencies and if they didn't pass—they didn't wrestle.

The coach kept shaking his head, but I had to admit that Mrs. Flanagan had a point. Eating ice cubes instead of a proper lunch is definitely not a great thing for your body.

Finally, the coach agreed with the nurse. They decided

to work out sensible diets for the boys on the wrestling team to follow if they were having trouble maintaining their weights. But under no circumstances would the coach force a wrestler down to a weight that might be unhealthy—not to mention dangerous—for him.

"Well," I stated as we left the office, "that's that."

"I am still surprised it was the nurse," Ollie said, leading the way out of the school.

"How'd you know she fixed the scale?" Nina asked curiously.

"Well, it was really just a hunch," I replied. "I mean, she had the opportunity—it was her scale after all—and then I realized she had the motive. Mrs. Flanágan yelled at Gina for not following a sensible diet, I overheard the phone conversation about the iron tests and I even tested the scale with the dumbbell. All I really needed was proof."

"That's all," Ollie said with a laugh. It's true, proof is everything. But I was sure that Mrs. Flanagan was behind it.

"Right," I replied. "So the coach and I decided to confront her. And Mrs. Flanagan crumbled."

"Like a dry cookie," Nina added.

I didn't say anything. I definitely preferred to ignore that bad joke.

"Hey, guys," Ollie said, opening the front door and stepping out onto the street. "All this talk about dieting has left me starving. Let's go to Kreagle's and pig out on ice cream!"

"Sounds good!" Nina agreed enthusiastically. "What do you say, Jack?"

"Sure," I replied. "And the only other thing I have to say is, 'Case closed!' "

About the Authors

K. B. Gardner is an enthusiastic sports fan and participant who currently resides in Arlington, Massachusetts. This is her first published story.

Leah Jerome loves sports—especially baseball and basketball. She has followed the Mets and the Knicks since she was nine and likes to go to at least one home game a season. Halfway to a Master's Degree in Education, Leah has written two other books. She lives in Ossining, New York.

Max Olson attends New York University where he is pursuing a B.A. in English with a specialization in creative writing. A writer since the sixth grade, Max began fencing while at Mamaroneck High School and he currently fences sabre for the NYU fencing team.

Creative Consultant

L. E. Wolfe, under various names, has created three young adult series, as well as authored a number of books. An editor of sports books for children and adults, she has also written for television. Ms. Wolfe lives in the Hudson Valley where she enjoys running and rollerblading.